OSLG

SINISTER ISLE OF LOVE

Jenny Carr is joining her brother on the Caribbean island of Taminga to start a new life. On her way, she meets Peter Blaine, a successful businessman on the island. He couldn't be more of a contrast to Craig Hannant, whose business is failing. His wife had died in mysterious circumstances, and Craig is now a difficult man to be around — but Jenny falls for Craig, despite all the signs that she is making the biggest mistake of her life . . .

Books by Phyllis Mallett
in the Linford Romance Library:

LOVE IN PERIL
THE TURNING POINT
LOVE'S MASQUERADE
POOR LITTLE RICH GIRL
ISLE OF INTRIGUE
HOUSE OF FEAR
DEADLY INHERITANCE
THE HEART IS TORN

PHYLLIS MALLETT

◆

SINISTER ISLE OF LOVE

Complete and Unabridged

LINFORD
Leicester

First published in Great Britain

First Linford Edition
published 2013

A catalogue record for this book is available
from the British Library.

ISBN 978–1–4448–1793–5

Published by
F. A. Thorpe (Publishing)
Anstey, Leicestershire

Set by Words & Graphics Ltd.
Anstey, Leicestershire
Printed and bound in Great Britain by
T. J. International Ltd., Padstow, Cornwall

This book is printed on acid-free paper

1

Excitement bubbled up inside her as Jenny Carr looked down at the sparkling, blue waters of the Caribbean. The airliner on which she was travelling was about to land at Kingston, and from there she would begin the last lap of her journey to the isle of Taminga, where her brother, Tim, managed the Hannant sugar cane plantation.

A twinge of sadness encroached upon her happiness as the reason for the trip came to mind. For years she had lived with her invalid father, taking care of him and working as a Staff Nurse at the local hospital. Then her father died, and when Tim came over for the funeral, he had insisted that she join him on Taminga to start a new life. She sighed. It had seemed impractical at first, but Tim had even secured a post for her at the British Hospital on the island, and so here she was — flying to a life that held the promise of fulfilment and happiness.

There had always been a kind of magic in her heart when she read of tropical islands, and now all this seemed like a dream. The break with England had not been as difficult as she imagined, for there was no-one back there she cared for. At twenty-four she'd never had a regular boy-friend, and had taken care of her father for as long as she could remember. His death had left a void in her heart, and she knew she needed a challenge in life to give her a reason for going on.

She leaned back in her seat and closed her eyes, permitting her past to drift across the screen of her mind. Her mother had died when she was ten years old, and her father's death had dealt her a great shock. This change should do exactly what her brother had envisaged, it would give her a new interest in life. England had seemed a harsh place, with its memories of worry and heartbreak, but this new world of sunshine and promise filled her with hope.

A stewardess warned that they were approaching Kingston, and Jenny opened her eyes and fastened her seat belt. She was filled with anticipation as the aeroplane swept down to land. The big wheels screeched on the runway, there was a jolt, and then a smooth run in to a standstill. Collecting her luggage, she passed through Customs, aware of a thudding sensation in her heart. She felt vibrantly alive for the first time in many years.

She caught a taxi outside the airport and was transported swiftly through the crowded streets to the hotel that Tim had booked her into. As she travelled, she looked around eagerly at the scenery, saw her first palm tree growing in its natural state, and gazed at the cheerful faces of the natives crowding the streets. The atmosphere was exotic, and she sensed that she would not be disappointed, however her future evolved.

At the hotel, she was shown to a room overlooking the bay, and a gasp of pleasure escaped her when she went to the window to look at the view. There was a stretch of vivid, blue sea and a narrow strip of yellow sand fringed with palm trees. Her blue eyes glinted as she devoured the sight, and she smiled happily. This was typical of the view her mind persisted in thrusting up whenever she had thought of this part of the world, and it was difficult to accept that she had finally arrived . . .

She was to leave by a local charter plane the next morning for Taminga, and this evening was hers to use for exploration. She was excited, agog to see everything, and after resting she changed and went sight-seeing. The time passed all too quickly, and when darkness fell, she began to feel the effects of her long journey. She returned thankfully to the hotel, and as the desk clerk handed over her key he leaned towards her conspiratorially.

'Mr Blaine, in Room Twelve, has asked to be advised of your return, Miss Carr,' he said.

'Mr Blaine?' Jenny frowned. 'There must be some mistake. I don't know anyone of that name.'

'He's a very important man on the island of Taminga,' the clerk added.

'Ah! Then perhaps my brother asked him to look me up.' Jenny smiled. 'Room Twelve, was it?'

'That's right, miss.'

Jenny took her key and went up to the first floor to knock on the door of Number Twelve. Her heart was beating a trifle faster than normal when the door was opened and a tall, athletic man gazed at her. He was well tanned, his brown eyes bright, his gaze penetrating.

'There's no need for you to introduce yourself,' he said before she could speak. 'Obviously you're Tim's sister, Jenny. Why, you and he might be twins.'

'Tim is a little older than me,' Jenny said. 'The clerk downstairs said you

5

were enquiring about me.'

'Yes.' He smiled, revealing perfect teeth. 'I'm Peter Blaine. When Tim learned that I'd be in Kingston on business when you arrived, he asked me to check on you. Have you everything you need?'

'Yes, thanks!' She nodded. 'I only arrived this afternoon. I've been out sightseeing.'

'I believe it's your first time in this part of the world, isn't it?' He smiled. 'No wonder your eyes are shining! I've been out here nearly fifteen years, but I can remember my first impressions. I hope you'll be happy on Taminga.'

'Thank you. I'm sure I shall!' Jenny was in no doubt about her future.

'It's a pity I didn't finish my business much earlier,' he said. 'I could have shown you around. But we'll be travelling on the same plane tomorrow, and I hope we shall become good friends, Jenny. May I call you Jenny?'

'Certainly!' She felt slightly over-whelmed by his friendliness, and decided that Tim must think highly of him to ask him to look her up.

'Tim and I are close friends,' he said, as if reading her thoughts. 'I own The Trade Wind Hotel on Taminga, and I expect we shall see a lot of one another later. Tim told me you plan to work at the local hospital.'

'Yes. I'm a fully qualified nurse,' Jenny confirmed. 'I'll be starting work at the hospital after a month's holiday on the island.'

He opened his door a little wider. 'Can I offer you a drink?'

'Thank you, but not tonight.' She shook her head gently. 'I'm so tired after all the travelling and excitement, I can hardly keep my eyes open.'

He nodded. 'OK! I'll see you to the airfield in the morning. We're travelling on the same flight. Be ready by nine. Good-night, and sleep well. I'll look forward to showing you the sights on Taminga.'

'Thank you.' Jenny was touched by his friendly manner.

Her feelings next morning when she awoke were a mixture of surprise and wonder. It would take her some time to grow accustomed to these exotic surroundings, she thought, gazing from the window at the picturesque bay. Her eyes narrowed against the glare of the sun. Then she had to push herself into activity, for time was passing relentlessly, and she was only just ready to face the world when there was a knock at the door.

Peter Blaine stood outside, dressed in an immaculate, white, linen suit. He smiled cheerfully, his dark eyes gleaming as he noted the vision she presented in a pale-yellow dress, her blonde hair piled on top of her shapely head.

'May I escort you to breakfast?' he asked. 'It's just over an hour before take-off.' He paused then and their eyes met. 'You're going to create quite a stir in Taminga, I warn you.'

'Compliments so early in the day?' she countered him lightly, her blue eyes glistening.

He smiled, and Jenny felt her heart lighten.

The airfield was nothing like the airport she had landed at the day before, and Jenny saw a small twin-engined aircraft awaiting them. Peter was on close terms with the pilot, and there were several other passengers. When the aircraft took off they flew south. This was the last lap of her journey! She had accepted Tim's word that she would love Taminga, and could only wait to see if she had really made the right choice.

The flight seemed long because Jenny was filled with growing excitement. The surface of the sea was broken with the dark formations of many islands, the whole panoramic view looking like a gigantic tapestry laid out for her inspection. Then Peter leaned towards her and pointed through the window.

'That dark speck on the horizon is Taminga,' he said.

Jenny watched the growing speck until it became the largest island she had yet seen. The aeroplane tilted and swung, changing her point of view, and she saw that the island consisted of two mountains, one slightly larger than the other. White surf glinted along parts of the coast, and yellow sand sparkled brightly against the dark blue of the sea and the lighter blue of the overlying sky.

'It's beautiful!' she said softly.

'It's even better at ground level,' he assured her.

The plane descended, and below and ahead of them Jenny saw an airstrip. She caught a glimpse of a clustered town to the south, with a small, enclosed harbour, and along the shore-line, that stretched away in a great curve, were many small dwellings clinging to points of vantage above the wavering shore.

'Do you see that small bay to the north?' Peter asked. He leaned across her to point through the porthole. 'Tim's bungalow is there, overlooking the harbour where most of the Hannant plantation's produce is shipped out. All that land in the valley between the mountains belong to the Hannant estate. It's the largest holding on the island.'

'Tim told me something about the estate,' Jenny said, gazing at the features on the ground. 'But I can't recall the name of the owner.'

'Craig Hannant!' There was a sudden rasp in Peter's tone that caused Jenny to glance quickly at him.

'He's a strange man, as no doubt you'll soon discover when you meet him. He's become something of a problem since his wife died. Tim practically runs the place now, and you can be proud of the way he has helped Hannant since his tragedy.'

Jenny watched the ground, determined to miss nothing. They were swooping down to land now, and she could make out details of the airstrip. There was a small building with several cars parked beyond it. Her breathing quickened as she experienced a sense of speed. Then they bumped gently onto grass and rolled towards the lone building, and a pang of unreality caught her as they alighted . . .

The first person Jenny saw was her sister-in-law, Debbie, standing at a rail in front of the building. They waved frantically to each other as Jenny hurried forward with Peter following in close attendance.

'Jenny! I'm so happy you're here at last!' Debbie was petite and dark-haired, with brown eyes and an expressive face. 'Did you have a good trip?'

'Debbie! It's been wonderful! And I'm so happy to be here! How are you?' Jenny dropped her case and hugged Debbie. The girls had always been close friends.

'How's Selina?' she demanded excitedly. 'I doubt if I'll be able to recognise her now!'

'She's fine!' Debbie smiled indulgently. 'I had quite a job getting her to school today because she knew you were coming.' Her dark eyes were alert as she studied Jenny's enrapt expression. 'I'm so glad to see you looking happy. It must have been dreadful for you alone in England.'

'It was! But that's all in the past now,' Jenny said gently.

'I met her in Kingston,' Peter intervened, coming forward. 'Tim asked me to look out for her.' He set down Jenny's luggage. 'How are you, Debbie?'

'Very well, thank you.' Debbie's voice changed abruptly, became cool, unfriendly. Jenny was somewhat shocked as her sister-in-law added, 'I'm sure Jenny would have managed all right on her own.'

'I'll leave her in your capable hands and take my leave, then.' Peter's smile showed that Debbie's manner had left him unmoved. 'It was a pleasure meeting you, Jenny.' He paused, then asked, 'May I call on you in a few days, when you've had the chance to settle in?'

'Yes. I'd like that,' Jenny told him. 'And thank you for taking the trouble to see me here safely.'

He smiled and took her hand briefly, then departed. Jenny gazed after him before looking at Debbie, who was regarding her intently.

'Don't you like him?' Jenny asked.

'He's a very likeable man!' Debbie countered. 'But he has a reputation, and the way he looks at you grates on my nerves.'

'I found him charming,' Jenny said. 'And I meet everyone with an open mind.'

Debbie smiled. 'Come on. Let's get your luggage into the car. I'll show you something of the island on the drive to the bungalow. Tim wanted to come and meet you but he's too busy to get away just now. He said he hoped you would understand.'

'Of course.' Jenny nodded. 'Peter was telling me something of Tim's work. He runs the whole estate now, doesn't he?'

'He does, and it takes a lot of running, believe me.' Debbie's profile was grim as she helped carry Jenny's luggage to the waiting car. 'Personally, I don't like the way things are shaping. If Tim isn't careful he may find himself out of a job.'

They left the airfield, chatting excitedly as Debbie drove along the coast road, and Jenny was delighted with what she saw. They entered the valley that lay between the two mountains, and Jenny's thoughts receded as she gazed, enthralled, at the rugged scenery. Debbie saw her interest and stopped the car at a spot overlooking the shore to point out their white-painted bungalow nestling among the palms on the opposite side of the bay.

'There's home!' she said proudly. 'You're sure to like it, Jenny. Just look at that view! And the sea! You'll adore the swimming!'

Jenny nodded as she looked around, and Debbie drove on through the valley. The car followed a track which led through a gateway. Trees grew densely around the bungalow, casting plenty of shade, and there were clusters of exotic flowers of many hues — hibiscus, bougainvillaea and frangipani. Debbie brought the car to a halt and they alighted. Jenny looked around appreciatively, her eyes recording every minutest detail, and she was aware that Debbie watched her closely for reaction, pride showing in her face.

'Wow, it's hot! But this is wonderful!' Jenny exclaimed.

'I knew you'd love the place,' Debbie said. 'Come inside now. It'll be a lot cooler. You must take things easy for a few days, to get acclimatised.'

The interior of the bungalow was, Jenny discovered, the last word in modern comfort. Debbie was justly filled with pride when she showed Jenny the bedroom she and Tim had prepared for her. It overlooked the bay, and the view from the window was beautiful. Jenny was vociferous in her praise.

Debbie smiled. 'Selina is worried that you won't like the island and will want to return to England,' she said. 'She's so excited about you coming.'

'How's she doing at school?' Jenny asked.

'For a six-year-old, very well! She wanted to have the day off today to come and meet you, but school must come first. And the first thing she'll want to do when she gets home is drag you down to the bay for a swim.'

'I can't find anything wrong with that plan,' Jenny countered.

'Well, first things first. Are you hungry?'

'Not at the moment, thanks. I'm too excited to care about anything as mundane as eating.'

'Let's have a cup of coffee then and you can relax. Selina won't be home until about five, so there's a couple of hours of peace left. I'm usually alone all day, which is why I'm so glad you've finally arrived. I shall have great pleasure showing you around, I can tell you.'

'Don't you get bored with so much time to yourself?' Jenny asked.

'Not really. There's always something

to do, somewhere to go.' Debbie smiled. 'And you'll never find time hanging on your hands when the local young men find out about you.'

They sat in the shade of the veranda and Jenny slowly relaxed. A sudden movement in the undergrowth nearby startled her.

An ageing native appeared, walking barefoot in the grass. He was attired in a pair of shorts that were in need of scrubbing, and his off-white vest was badly holed. However, his fleshy face was creased with a wide grin as he paused on the bottom step of the veranda, his quick, brown eyes flickering from Jenny to Debbie as he took a bulging, canvas bag from his shoulder and set it down.

'Afternoon, ladies,' he greeted in a pleasant, sing-song voice. 'I brought some fish for the oven.'

'Hello, Rube,' Debbie replied. 'Put half a dozen in the cold box, will you?'

She glanced at Jenny. 'This is Rube Binder. He's the best fisherman on the island. Rube, this is Tim's sister, Jenny. She's planning to live here.'

'I am pleased to meet you, Miss Jenny.' Rube bobbed his head emphatically. 'I hope you like it here.' He turned away abruptly, but glanced back over his shoulder and grinned at Jenny. 'See you around.'

'He's quite a character,' Debbie said, 'Selina adores him, and he's often down in the bay with her. He swims like a fish, and is at least ten years older than he looks.'

The sound of an approaching vehicle stopped conversation, and Jenny looked eagerly towards the path.

'That sounds like Tim's Land-Rover,' Debbie said. 'I asked him to try and get home early to see you.'

Jenny got to her feet when a Land-Rover appeared, and her excitement grew when she recognised her brother's smiling face behind the wheel. He stopped the vehicle and sprang out, and Jenny ran towards him, hurling herself into his embrace.

'Hello, Sis,' he said gently. 'It's so good to see you! And you're looking very well! What kind of a trip did you have?'

'Great!' Jenny took his arm and walked him to where Debbie was standing on the edge of the veranda. 'And I'm so happy to be here at last. It's a marvellous place. I can hardly wait to start exploring.'

'I'm glad your first impressions are good.' His pale, blue eyes were glinting with pleasure. 'I'm going to try and make time during the next week or so to show you around and make sure you settle in. All your bad days have been left behind in England, and it won't take you long to forget them. You're here now and this is a new life. We're all that's left of the Carr family, and you're going to see the best of it out here.'

He kissed her again affectionately, then threw his free arm around Debbie. Jenny looked up into his tanned face, saw his happiness at her presence, and felt her own heart lighten. She realised that she had missed him, but now they were together again and that was all that mattered. The future would be a great success, she sensed, and was determined that nothing would change it.

2

Debbie was silent for some moments after Tim left to go back to the plantation, evidently still thinking of him. Then she moved impatiently and looked at Jenny, shaking her head and heaving a sigh.

'I don't know what to make of Craig Hannant these days,' she said. 'He seems to be getting worse instead of better. I thought he would have got over his troubles by now, but he doesn't make the effort to forget the past.'

'You mentioned that his wife died,' Jenny ventured. 'Is that why he's let his life go to pot?'

'You could put it like that.' Debbie nodded grimly. 'I always felt sorry for Craig, but it's useless trying to help him. When we ask him here he more often than not fails to turn up, and on the rare occasions he does come he's usually been drinking. In fact, some of our friends are beginning to stay away to avoid him. There's a limit to what you can do for a man who doesn't want to be helped. It's Tim I feel sorry for, though. Working for a man like Craig, he has to be on his toes all the time.'

'Why is Craig Hannant so broken up?' Jenny asked. 'Is it because he's lost his wife's guiding hand?'

'That could be the reason! But they didn't get along too well before their troubles started. She wasn't the type to be a planter's wife, although Craig never accepted that! Ann hated the island, and treated the locals as if they were dirt. There was a scandal once when she took a whip to one of the field hands. She belonged to the past, and her end was a relief to a great many people.' Debbie saw the shock that came to Jenny's face and shook her head slowly. 'That sounded harsh, I admit, but I can't help it, Jenny. Ann tried to have an affair with Tim when she first came here. She was always trying to involve someone! Luckily, Tim isn't the type but she never forgave him for holding out against her. He doesn't know I know, and I'm very proud of your brother. I'd do anything for him. He's handling quite a thankless job at the moment.'

Jenny nodded. 'What happened to Ann Hannant?' she asked.

'She drove over a cliff one night during a storm.' Debbie spoke harshly. 'It was called an accident, but I've always had my doubts.'

'Do you mean she might have been murdered?' Jenny was horrified.

'I hesitate to put a name to it, but if it wasn't accidental then what other explanation could there be?' Debbie stood up. 'I think you should take a rest now. You're looking a bit hot and bothered, and you must be careful until you've acclimatised.'

Jenny nodded, relieved to be able to rest. She went to her room and lay down, but when she closed her eyes she could not sleep for impressions and snatches of conversation began buzzing around in her mind. Then she drifted into slumber, until Selina Carr came running into the bungalow in search of her. She was hardly able to get to her feet before the girl was in her arms, hugging her tightly and thrusting her excited face against Jenny's.

'Aunt Jenny, I'm so glad to see you! Mummy said you'd be here when I came home but I didn't really believe her. And the day has been ever so long.'

'Selina,' Jenny exclaimed. 'Stand down a moment and let me look at you!' She smiled as she released the girl, who stepped back and danced a pirouette so Jenny could inspect her. 'How you've grown! Why, you're a young lady now.'

'I was only four the last time you saw me,' Selina said, her brown eyes glinting with pleasure. 'You're going to stay with us until you go to work at the hospital, aren't you?'

'Yes, dear. I have a month's holiday before I take up my post. And we'll have some fun together, Selina, I promise you!'

'Can we go swimming after tea?' Selina demanded as they went into the kitchen where Debbie was busy, and she clapped her hands when Jenny agreed. 'I knew we would have fun when you came!' she declared. 'Mummy always has something else to do when I want her to go with me!'

'Mothers are pretty busy sometimes!' Debbie cut in, smiling. 'But we do have lots of fun, Selina, and you know it! Now go and change your clothes. You've got Jenny living here until she goes to work at the hospital. On Sunday, perhaps we can take her on a picnic up the mountain. I'm sure she won't believe that around here orchids grow like weeds.'

'Now you're pulling my leg!' Jenny retorted with a smile.

'It's true, Aunt Jenny, it really is!' Selina cried excitedly, before hurrying from the room.

'She's certainly grown since I saw her

last, Debbie,' Jenny said. 'She must be very good company for you now.'

'She is, but you mustn't let her run you off your feet, you know. And don't let her monopolise your time.'

There was a knock at the door and Debbie excused herself. She left the room and Jenny arose and moved to the window to look at the exotic vegetation that was growing densely just outside the window. She heard Debbie's voice outside, and then her sister-in-law reappeared, followed by a tall man.

'Jenny, this is Frank Carter — Doctor Carter,' Debbie introduced. 'You'll be working with him when you take up your duties at the hospital.'

'I was passing and thought I'd look in to see if you had arrived,' Frank Carter said, crossing the room with extended hand. The handshake he gave her was firm and friendly. 'I'm pleased to meet you, Jenny, and I sincerely hope you'll be happy working with us. We're one big, happy family at the hospital.'

'How do you do, Doctor?' Jenny

responded, thinking what a pleasant man he seemed. 'I've been looking forward to meeting you, and I shall be coming to the hospital in a day or two to look around. I can't wait to take up my duties.'

'I like your enthusiasm.' He smiled. He was not old. Jenny did not think he had reached forty. His face was tanned from years in the sun and his hair had a bleached look about it. 'Come and see us by all means and I'll have the pleasure of showing you around. But enjoy yourself while you can and settle in. This is your first time on the island, isn't it?'

'It is.' Jenny nodded.

'Then you have a lot of pleasure in store. I'm sure you'll like it here, and you won't find better colleagues anywhere.' He smiled again warmly. 'Sorry I'm in such a hurry, but I have to leave now. We're always so very busy. I'll show you around when you come to see us.'

'Thank you,' Jenny said gratefully.

When she awoke the next morning, Jenny instinctively looked out of the window to see if the weather was wet, and the sight of exotic scenery brought a smile to her face. She really had arrived! It wasn't all a dream! She looked at her watch, saw the time was after eight. Pulling on her dressing gown, she left the room to seek Debbie and found a local girl cleaning the lounge.

'Hello, I am Aya,' the girl greeted. 'I come each morning to clean the house.'

'Hello, Aya, I'm Jenny.'

'I have been told about you. Do you like the island?'

'Very much!' Jenny smiled. 'Where's Debbie?'

'She take Miss Selina to the road to catch her ride to school.'

'I see! Well, I'd better get dressed.' Jenny turned to the door.

'You are to work at the hospital, I hear.' Aya spoke good English, her accent sounding quaint and attractive.

'Yes. I'm a nurse.' Jenny paused.

'Then you must be very clever. But Mr Tim is clever. He saves Master Craig much trouble. Mr Tim works hard, and I hope he can make Master Craig change his mind.'

'Change his mind?' Jenny turned to face the girl. 'What do you mean, Aya?'

'Master Craig is thinking of selling the plantation and returning to England.'

'Really!' Jenny frowned. 'Tim didn't mention that.'

'Then perhaps you'll forget I did, but word has gone round the island, and it doesn't take long for everyone to know.'

Jenny nodded and left the room. She was thoughtful as she showered and then dressed. When she returned to the lounge, Debbie was in there and Aya had gone.

'Hello, Jenny. Did you sleep well?' Debbie enquired.

'I've never spent a more comfortable night!'

'I expect you were tired out by travelling. What would you like to do today? Shall we drive into town and look around or would you prefer to leave that for another day? We could go north along the coast road. It circles the entire island, and the scenery has to be seen to be believed.'

'Anything you say,' Jenny responded.

'Well, Tim says I'm to make sure you don't get lonely or bored, and his word is law as far as I'm concerned.'

'You make him sound like a feudal lord!'

'He's all right.' Debbie paused and considered. 'Would you like to look round the Hannant plantation? We could drive to Craig's place and I'll show you over it. Craig won't mind. In any case, I don't expect he'll be there. He lives in town most of the time these days. We might see Tim, though, and perhaps he'll be able to spend a little time with us.'

'That sounds like a good idea,' Jenny agreed.

'I'll get the car out. Aya will make us a packed lunch. Did you meet her?'

'Yes. She's quite friendly.'

'Just so long as you don't get any ideas about Craig!' Debbie warned. 'Aya lives on the plantation, and I suspect she's madly in love with Craig.'

'Really?' Jenny was interested.

'Oh, he doesn't know she exists! And I'm certain Aya would cut off her right arm for him. That's the way these island girls are. They show their emotions far more than us.'

The morning was exhilarating as they drove inland along a narrow, dusty road. Jenny gazed around with eyes that were ready to see beauty everywhere. Fields occupied the valley, reaching up to the lower slopes of the mountains. Then she saw a large, white house, built in colonial style, which stood alone on rising ground like a sentinel of the mountain. Debbie stopped the car, smiling as she watched for Jenny's reaction.

'If you're reacting as I did the first time I set eyes on Craig's house then you're feeling pretty good right now,' she said. 'I always thought this place was too good for Ann Hannant, and I'm not being catty when I say that. I gained the impression that she was intent upon dragging Craig down, and the plantation has certainly started to go to the dogs, despite Tim's efforts.'

'So what are Craig's intentions?' Jenny enquired as they continued.

'I wish I knew what was in his mind! Tim is very worried. If Craig does sell up, the new people might think Tim is at fault for the state the plantation is in. It's always the manager who is responsible and takes the blame.'

Jenny was thoughtful as they drove into the front yard of the big house, and Debbie uttered an exclamation when she saw Craig's car there.

'He would be here!' she muttered. 'Never mind. He won't mind us looking around. He's proud of the place despite the way he's treating it now.'

Jenny felt reluctant to thrust herself uninvited upon a man of Craig Hannant's apparent disposition, and her heart seemed to miss a beat when a man suddenly appeared in the doorway of the house as they approached it.

He was tall and powerfully built, no more than thirty years old, she judged, and had obviously kept himself in good, physical condition. His face was impassive, though, as he looked first at Debbie, then at Jenny. He was gaunt, and his dark eyes showed that he'd had little sleep. His manner seemed to exude aggression.

Jenny felt a trickle of emotion seep through her as she gazed at him. His face was not a stranger's, she told herself, frowning, because she had never met him before in her life. Yet she had an uncanny feeling that she had known him before somewhere, and the sensation persisted as they halted and looked at him.

'Sightseeing?' he demanded.

'Yes, Craig.' Debbie made a half-hearted attempt to be friendly. 'And your house was the first place I wanted Jenny to see. Do you mind?'

He shook his head. 'Not at all. You

can set fire to it if you wish!' He came down the half-dozen steps to confront them, his narrowed eyes searching Jenny's face. 'Am I to assume that this is Tim's sister?' he demanded. 'Aren't you going to introduce us, Debbie?'

'Certainly!' Debbie grimaced. 'Jenny Carr, Craig Hannant.'

'How do you do?' He spoke formally, and before Jenny could reply he had stepped around her and walked to his car, calling back across his shoulder. 'Sorry, but I'm in a hurry. And you know where everything is, Debbie. Help yourselves to anything you want.' He paused and looked once more at Jenny, who moistened her lips, her heart unaccountably racing.

'Thank you, Craig,' Debbie replied, 'but we just want to look.'

Jenny watched intently as Craig got into his big car and drove away. He made the dust fly along the road, and took the top bend at tremendous speed, his tyres squealing a protest that echoed over the fields and grated across Jenny's nerves. After the car had vanished she realised she was holding her breath, and there was a tension in her mind she had never before experienced. Glancing at Debbie, she discovered that the girl was looking at her.

Debbie sighed and turned towards the house. 'Come and have a look around while you can. Let's see what sort of a mess he's making inside.'

Jenny entered the house with the sense of awe that comes to most people entering a cathedral for the first time. She was strangely disconcerted by the realisation that Craig Hannant had affected her. She felt sympathy towards Craig Hannant, she realised, and the knowledge left her feeling uneasy.

Later, when Debbie drove into town, Jenny was immediately taken by the beauty of the place. They walked along the quayside, and there was so much to see that Jenny's eyes ached from the glare of the sun and the myriad of colour that surrounded her. Jenny was enrapt as they sauntered around, while

Debbie kept up a running commentary on what was happening.

'We'll have lunch in the Trade Wind Hotel,' Debbie suggested as they left the harbour and began a tour of the town.

'That's Peter Blaine's place, isn't it?' Jenny enquired.

'Yes. I thought you'd like to see the kind of place he's got.' Debbie's eyes clouded as she gazed at Jenny. 'I feel guilty about this because I had decided to keep you away from Peter at all costs. I don't want to be the one to put you into contact with him.'

'That sounds ominous,' Jenny observed. 'You really dislike him, don't you?'

'Not dislike!' Debbie shook her head. 'Distrust, perhaps. Peter's name was linked with Ann Hannant's at one time, and her death left an unsavoury atmosphere over the whole island. I suppose it's because no-one really knows exactly what happened the night she died, but her death has put a cloud over Peter and another over Craig.

37

Peter is generally quite nice, and very good company, but there could be a darker side to him.'

'I can take care of myself,' Jenny said softly. 'But we'll eat where ever you say, Debbie. It doesn't really matter.'

They went into the Trade Wind Hotel and Peter Blaine appeared as if he had been informed of their arrival. He was charming, determined to play the perfect host to Jenny, who studied him critically in the light of what Debbie had said about him as he escorted them to a table and insisted upon joining them despite Debbie's coolness.

He was certainly a handsome man, Jenny decided, aware that his smooth manner could flatter and overwhelm a girl. She found herself liking him instinctively, despite Debbie's warnings, and was prepared to accept the promptings of her intuition for they had never betrayed her in the past.

'How are you settling in, Jenny?' he enquired, pouring wine for them.

'Very well, thank you,' she replied.

'I'm going to love it here.'

'So you've already decided to stay!' His gaze was pure magic. 'I'm glad to hear that! When may I call on you?' His gaze slid to Debbie's face. 'I haven't been a regular caller at your place in recent months, but I hope to remedy that now.'

'Call whenever you wish,' Debbie said slowly. 'It's up to Jenny if she wants to ask friends along. Our home is her home.'

'Good!' He nodded, a gleam of satisfaction in his level gaze. 'What are you doing this evening, Jenny?'

'I haven't made arrangements to do anything,' she replied.

'Then may I take you out? The Carib Club overlooks Heron Bay, and I'd like to be the one who first takes you there. I'm one of the directors, and we have every game imaginable, from bingo to roulette. You'll really enjoy it.'

'Thank you, I'd like to accept,' she said quietly, then added, 'Unless Tim has made any arrangements that I don't know about?'

'He hasn't,' Debbie replied. 'He told me this morning that he would leave it up to you, Jenny. We don't usually go out much during the week because Tim is so tired when he finishes work.'

'Then I'll call for you at about seven-thirty,' Peter said with a smile. 'It's not far from your bungalow to Heron Bay.'

They had lunch, and afterwards Peter was obviously reluctant to let Jenny go. When he finally showed them out to the street he caught hold of Jenny's hand and squeezed it gently.

'Until this evening,' he said softly. 'You'll meet everyone who is anyone at the Club. It will start you off right with the people who matter. I was going to telephone you this afternoon to see if you would be interested in coming along, so I'm really pleased you showed up when you did.'

'I'll be ready at seven-thirty,' Jenny responded. 'Thank you.'

Debbie sighed as they walked on to see the parts of the town they had not as yet explored. Jenny sensed that her sister-in-law did not approve of her decision to go out with Peter Blaine, but the girl would not remark upon it. They entered the older part of the town, and Jenny became engrossed in her surroundings as they wandered through the narrow streets. Debbie was somewhat subdued, and it was not long before she intimated that she was tired.

'But I'm more concerned about you,' she said by way of excuse. 'You mustn't overdo it. The heat will take its toll, and if you're going out with Peter this evening you'd better rest this afternoon. And don't let him keep you out all night. You'll need to work up to that very slowly.'

'You don't really like the idea of me going out with him, do you?' Jenny asked.

Debbie shrugged. 'He's probably OK. I just can't help believing the stories I've heard about him. I'd hate

41

you to get hurt, Jenny.'

Jenny was tired by the time they reached the bungalow, and didn't protest when Debbie suggested she lie down for a rest. The heat had worn her out, she discovered, and sleep came to her the moment she closed her eyes.

3

At seven that evening, Jenny was filled
with an unnatural tension, and even
Debbie's assurances that she looked
beautiful in her blue, silk shift could not
remove the pangs of anticipation that
gripped her. Tim hadn't arrived home
by the time Peter called, and Jenny said
goodbye to Debbie with an apologetic
tone in her voice.

'Have a nice time,' Debbie said,
escorting her to the door. 'And take
good care of her, Peter.'

'I will,' he replied with a smile. 'I
haven't seen anyone so beautiful in a
long time, I can tell you. There will be
some very envious men at the Club
tonight!'

'I hope Tim won't mind me running
off like this,' Jenny said as Peter opened
his car door for her.

'Of course he won't,' Debbie retorted.

'You're on holiday, Jenny, and you may not get many chances to enjoy yourself when you start nursing.'

Jenny waved to Debbie as the car pulled away, and then settled back in her seat and prepared to enjoy the evening.

When they arrived at the Carib Club she was astounded by the sight which it presented. Standing three stories high on a massive outcrop of cliff overlooking Heron Bay, it would not have been out of place on the Riviera. Its exterior was of dazzling white stone, and rows upon rows of shining windows punctuated the smooth walls.

'It was built for tourists,' Peter explained. 'But a growing number of islanders are using its amenities, and twenty-five percent belongs to me.'

'I'm impressed,' Jenny said with a smile.

'Come in and you'll see just what an enterprise it is.' He was obviously pleased with her reaction.

The interior substantiated the impressions gained from outside. Money had been no object in the building of this holiday playground, and Jenny wondered what kind of people were attracted during the high season. They were received by a head-waiter hovering near the doorway to the restaurant, and she sensed that their visit had been specially arranged for they were ushered to a reserved corner table that was half concealed by shrubs and plants. A small orchestra was playing in an elevated alcove, and Jenny was surprised by the number of people present.

The meal was exquisite, and Peter played host with great panache, a role which suited him admirably. After dinner he suggested they visit the gaming rooms. He led her casually along the wide corridors, all the furnishings showing the same high degree of luxury.

'Would you like to gamble?' Peter enquired. It was obvious that he was trying to dazzle her with his business, and she felt a little heady when he pushed dozens of expensive chips into her hands.

'I've never gambled before,' she declared.

'I'll show you what to do!' He led her to a vacant seat at a roulette table, then stood by her side. The croupier spoke in French. Peter pushed some chips across the table to cover number thirteen, and Jenny listened to the click of the ball and the spinning of the wheel as she glanced around at the intent faces of the gamblers. Peter lost, and gave a wry smile as Jenny looked at him.

'Go ahead,' he urged. 'Enjoy yourself. I have to see to something, but I won't be long, and they'll look after you. If you lose your stake then ask for the manager and tell him you are with me.'

He departed before Jenny could protest, and she glanced down at the pile of chips before her. They represented a small fortune, and she wondered that Peter could afford to throw away so much just to impress her. She played the game, gambling sparingly, and was elated when her number came up on the third spin. The croupier pushed a large pile of chips in front of her and she clenched her hands in excitement.

Peter returned eventually, and nodded approvingly when he saw that she had added to the original pile of chips.

'You're a natural!' he insisted. 'It is pure luck, you know, and some people have it, although most do not. Keep your winnings.'

'But these chips belong to you,' Jenny said firmly. 'I can't take it.'

He smiled. 'Doesn't it make you feel good, gambling with my money?' He sorted through the pile, removing the amount he had originally given her. 'There you are, if you're feeling independent. That's your winnings. Keep playing and see if you can increase it. I'll play with my pile.'

Jenny felt uncomfortable but she continued playing, and was relieved when she eventually lost all her winnings. Peter lost as well, and smiled as Jenny rose from the table.

'So you're not a born gambler!' he

commented, taking her arm and leading her from the big room. 'But perhaps that's just as well. I could be in trouble if you became hooked.'

'Gambling isn't for me,' she affirmed.

He led her out to a balcony that overlooked the sea. The moon was full, seemingly suspended just above the horizon, and the stars were so bright she could hardly believe they were real. A perfumed breeze caressed the balcony, and Jenny realised that she had not experienced a more beautiful night.

'This is the perfect setting for you,' Peter said gently. The muted sound of dance music was rising from a lower floor. 'This is a private balcony so we shan't be disturbed. Sit down and tell me if you are enjoying yourself.'

'I'm having a wonderful time,' she responded, gazing out to sea. The moon was casting a silver pathway across the surface of the bay which looked as if it led up to Heaven itself. 'I've never seen anything so beautiful.'

'And neither have I!' he retorted,

taking hold of her hand.

Jenny was unable to see him clearly in the moonlight, but he gained attractiveness from the shadows that surrounded them, and Jenny felt her senses wavering under the tropical assault being made upon them. If he was trying to impress her then he was greatly succeeding, she told herself.

'I hope we're going to be very good friends, Jenny,' he said, and she sensed his seriousness and stiffened a little. He gripped her hand tighter and slid towards her on the seat, a strong hand easing behind her to rest lightly against her shoulder blades. She instantly felt threatened, and drew a deep breath which she exhaled in a long sigh.

'Are you enjoying yourself?' he enquired yet again.

'Yes, very much so,' she replied.

'That's good to know!' He edged closer, his hand at her back drawing her towards him. 'I've had the feeling, for years, that I've been waiting around for a very important girl to appear in my life, and something tells me you are the girl.'

Jenny stiffened, momentarily shocked by his boldness.

'You haven't known me more than a few hours!' she gasped.

'What is time?' he countered, now very close. He pulled her into his embrace and his lips touched hers. Jenny started nervously and instinctively began to push him away.

'Please,' she begged. 'Don't spoil a wonderful evening.'

She knew instantly that she had said the wrong thing by the way he drew back from her. He gazed into her eyes, his face tense, his eyes glistening. Then he made an effort to relax and exhaled deeply. Arising, he grasped her hands and drew her erect, peering into her face.

'Don't these surroundings get to you?' he demanded.

'Did you bring me here this evening just to test me?' she countered.

'I'm a romantic at heart!' He

50

shrugged. 'Sorry if I move too swiftly for you. That's the way life is on the island, but remember this evening.'

'I certainly will,' she replied truthfully, but she did not mean it the way he hoped for the experience had served only to inform her that he could never become the man of her dreams. His kiss had succeeded only in producing another man's face in her mind — Craig Hannant — and it was that knowledge which filled her with such strong feelings. Somehow, she was being attracted to a man who was a stranger and hardly knew she existed.

* * *

The next morning, Jenny awoke early, and when she went out to the kitchen she was prepared for the inevitable fusillade of questions that Debbie would want to ask. She smiled at the eagerness and concern in Debbie's tone, and quickly put her at ease.

'No,' she said quietly. 'Peter didn't

ring any bells for me. It was patently obvious that he was keen to impress me, but all he succeeded in doing was make me aware that he's not my type.'

She did not add that her mind was plagued by Craig Hannant, and such was Debbie's relief, her sister-in-law let the subject drop. They had breakfast together, and then Debbie broached the subject of Jenny's day.

'I haven't given a thought to it,' Jenny said. 'Can we go out together?'

'No such luck!' Debbie said sorrowfully. 'Unfortunately, I have a circle of local wives calling this morning, and I'll be lucky if they leave before Selina gets home from school. I wouldn't want to inflict them on you, Jenny, so my car is outside, if you wish to use it. I'm sorry I can't be with you today, but it's just one of those things. We wives take it in turns to play hostess, and if it wasn't my turn I could have cried off, but they'll be descending on me, just like a plague of locusts, about mid-morning.'

'I certainly wouldn't want to get

caught up in that,' Jenny said teasingly. 'If you don't mind, I'll go into town and visit the hospital.'

'That's a good idea.' Debbie was relieved as she produced the car keys. 'I had visions of you sitting around here all day being bored to tears. If you like, I'll drive you into town and drop you at the hospital. Then, when Selina gets home from school, I could bring her and come and pick you up.'

'Fine.' Jenny smiled. 'I'd appreciate it if you drove because I'm a bit out of practice behind the wheel.'

The road was narrow and twisting, following the ever-changing shoreline edging the bay, and from time to time Debbie's attention wavered as she indicated points of interest she wished Jenny to see. They were travelling around a long bend when Debbie pointed to the distant shore, and as Jenny looked away from the road a large, black car came sweeping around the bend from the opposite direction.

Debbie cried out in shock and

instinctively steered for the side of the road. Luckily, they were not travelling fast, and left the road without trouble, but the approaching car was speeding, and swerved frighteningly as the driver applied his brakes. Jenny saw the vehicle scrape the opposite verge and then bounce back to the middle of the road. It passed their car with only inches to spare, tyres screeching a protest, before ramming a low bank and halting abruptly. The driver hung over the steering wheel as if he had been injured.

For a few shocked moments, there was a ghastly silence. Jenny sat frozen, looking over her shoulder at the other car. Then her shock receded and she sprang out of the vehicle to go running along the road, with Debbie following closely. She was breathless when she reached the black car, and instinctively leaned across the inert driver to switch off the ignition. Then she grasped hold of the man's shoulders and eased him back in the seat. Her hands began to tremble when she realised it was Craig Hannant.

'Is he hurt?' Debbie asked, her voice high-pitched and nervous.

'I don't know yet. Can you get round to the other side and help me lift him? He's unconscious.'

Debbie obeyed without question, and they managed to get Craig back from the steering wheel. Jenny kneeled on the seat to examine him, and discovered a large bump on his tanned forehead, which was oozing droplets of blood. There didn't seem to be any other injuries, and she was relieved. Debbie stared at her across the width of the seat.

'The fool!' she said emphatically. 'One of these days someone will be killed because of his driving. He almost had us this time, Jenny!'

Jenny did not reply. She was looking at Craig's face. He was groaning softly now, and she lifted his head slightly, trying to make him comfortable. Debbie got out of the car and came around to Jenny's side.

The dazed eyes that stared up at Jenny were pale blue, and she saw shock in his face as Craig Hannant recovered consciousness and tried to recall what had happened. Then he saw Jenny and a shadow crossed his harsh features. He stiffened, struggling to sit up despite her restraining hand upon his shoulder.

'Don't try to move for a few moments, Mr Hannant,' she said sharply. 'You've taken a nasty blow on the head and you're concussed, but you'll be all right if you do as you're told.'

'Get away!' He was not yet in control of his faculties, and Jenny was aware that his mind must be playing him tricks. 'You're dead, Ann!' he gasped, 'And I want you to stay that way.'

He tried to sit up but the effort proved to be too much for him and he fell sideways, his weight tugging Jenny forward as she tried to hold him.

'He thought you were his wife,'

Debbie gasped. 'And what a thing to say!'

'You can't take any notice of what a person in shock says,' Jenny said firmly. 'Forget his words, Debbie. Help me get him out of the car. If we lie him on the grass he'll get some air.'

They struggled with the heavy body and finally succeeded in getting Craig out of the car. Within moments he stirred again, and Jenny felt strangely touched as she gazed down into his pale, handsome face. She trembled when he suddenly grasped her hand and clung to it.

When Craig had recovered sufficiently, he shook his head in disbelief, and Jenny, watching him closely, saw bewilderment in his eyes.

'What happened?' he demanded huskily. 'Was anyone hurt?'

'Only you!' Debbie said sharply, her anger surprising Jenny. 'And it was only because I was able to react quickly that we weren't hurt. If I hadn't got out of your way you would have collided with us! I've never seen such bad driving, Craig! You should be banned from the roads! And it's not the first time you've come close to being involved in an accident!'

'All right, don't give me a dog's life!' His eyes were filled with shock and irritation. He was looking at Jenny, and a frown touched his face. 'Who are you?' he demanded. 'I don't recall seeing you before.'

'This is Tim's sister, Jenny,' Debbie cut in. 'And you met her yesterday. Don't you remember? Anyway, she's a fully-trained nurse so you're in good hands! But you very nearly killed her!'

'I'm sorry!' He sighed, his gaze remaining on Jenny. 'You're very like Tim,' he observed. 'I'm sure I would have known you without an introduction under normal circumstances. I hope you'll like Taminga.'

'Thank you,' Jenny responded. 'I'm sure I shall! But how are you feeling now? Can you get to your feet?'

'I expect so.' He started to rise, and

Jenny took hold of his arm as he staggered and almost reeled off balance.

'Have you been drinking, Craig?' Debbie demanded suspiciously.

'No, I haven't.' He spoke defensively, and Jenny frowned. His eyes were revealing inner pain. His wife had died in mysterious circumstances, and obviously the business was having a detrimental effect upon him. 'Thanks for your help,' he continued. 'You can leave me now. I'll sit in the car until my head clears, and I'll try to drive more carefully in future.'

'You've said that before,' Debbie retorted angrily. 'It's not good enough, Craig. If you're set upon killing yourself, that's your business. But you should choose a method that cannot involve innocent people.'

'Who said I'm trying to kill myself?' he demanded.

'You act as if you are intent upon it,' Debbie snapped. 'If you're not, then it's time you went back to riding a horse.'

He smiled cynically and turned to his

car. Jenny watched him closely. He seemed to be in full command of his senses but she was quite worried, and grasped Debbie's arm as her sister-in-law turned away. They watched him start the car and reverse slowly from the bank. Once clear, he alighted to check for damage. The front number plate was bent, but that was the only damage sustained, and he shrugged his shoulders and got back into the car.

'Thanks for your help,' he called, lifting a hand in acknowledgement. His face was ghastly pale, and Jenny grasped Debbie's arm.

'I can't let him go like this,' she said sharply. 'He's concussed. He could lose consciousness again at any moment. We must stop him.'

'Where are you going, Craig?' Debbie called as they went towards the car.

'Into town.'

'Then perhaps you'll give Jenny a lift. I have to get back home.'

He gazed at Jenny for a moment, then nodded slowly. 'All right, get in,' he said. 'I'll try and drive carefully.'

'I'll see you later,' Debbie said. 'Ring me when you can, Jenny.'

Jenny nodded and hurried around the car to get in at Craig's side. He glanced at her, his eyes slightly unfocused.

'I think it would be a good idea if I drove,' she said firmly.

'I'm all right,' he countered sharply. 'If you're afraid for yourself then you don't have to ride with me.'

'I want to get you to hospital for a check-up,' Jenny said firmly, 'and arguing about it will do you no good at all.'

'I'm all right, I tell you.' He shook his head emphatically, then groaned and put his hands to his temples. His face turned pale and he leaned back in his seat.

'You're an obstinate man, Mr Hannant!' Jenny told him sharply. 'And you're acting like a little boy! Now, perhaps, you'll do as I say.' She opened her door and slid out. 'Come on, move over and I'll drive,' she insisted, and by the time she had walked around the car, he had slid across into the front passenger seat. Jenny got into the driving seat, and her heart seemed to miss a beat as she looked into his face. He was lounging back, his eyes closed, and she took hold of his wrist and checked his pulse. He pulled his hand away, and she slammed the door and took stock of the driving controls.

She managed to get the car moving and drove towards the town, her nerves on edge until she became accustomed to the controls. From time to time she glanced at his immobile figure, and was determined to take him straight to the hospital, but when they reached the town he opened his eyes and sat up. A glance around gave him his bearings and he nodded.

'Good. Turn right, down there to the quay. I've got to go to my estate on the isle of Panaga. It's a four hour trip.'

'You must go to hospital first,' Jenny warned.

'Nothing doing!' He shook his head. 'I have some important business to attend to. You wouldn't want me to lose my estate here on Taminga, would you? Tim would be out of a job if I did.'

'I don't know if you're telling the truth or raving,' she countered.

'I do rave quite a lot a times,' he admitted. 'But this time I have to move fast.'

'You were certainly moving fast when you almost collided with us.' Jenny permitted a stern note to enter her voice. 'Are you tired of life? The roads on the island weren't built for such speed.'

'Turn there!' He ignored her observation, leaning forward to check for a parking place on the crowded quay. 'There. Turn in there and pull up.' He was holding a hand to his right temple, and Jenny could see dried blood on his forehead around the large bruise he had sustained.

'I do wish you'd go to the hospital for a check-up,' she said worriedly.

63

'Don't worry about me,' he retorted. 'I'll be all right. It will take more than a little knock to keep me down. But what are we going to do with you now? Are you doing anything special today?'

'Not at all. I was going to look around town until Debbie picks me up this afternoon.'

'There's nothing in this place to occupy you for more than an hour, let alone all day. You'd better come with me. In fact I may need your help on the trip. I'm not feeling too good. You could steer the boat if I need to lie down.'

'Well, I don't know about that!' Jenny said slowly. 'For one thing I'd need to let Debbie know my whereabouts.'

'There's a radio telephone on my boat. You can call her on that. Come on, let's get under way. Running into you on the road has put me behind my schedule.'

'It almost put you into hospital, and very nearly into your coffin,' she countered.

He laughed and got out of the car.

Jenny hurried to join him, and her pulses were racing as she accompanied him along the quay. They boarded a large, white-painted cabin cruiser, and Craig motioned for her to sit under the shade of the stern awning.

'I'll take her out to the open sea and then you can steer while I get cleaned up down below,' he said.

'I've never steered a boat before,' she retorted crisply.

'Well, she won't bite you,' he said tartly. 'And I'll show you what to do. You're not one of those females who can't turn her hand to anything, are you?' His eyes glinted as he gazed at her.

'I'm a fully-qualified nurse!' Jenny said sharply. 'Which should tell you a great deal, Mr Hannant.'

'We're going out through the gap in the reef.' He grasped her arm and led her to one side, and Jenny's eyes widened when she saw the huge waves that were smashing upon the obdurate reef in the distance.

'We're going out through that?' she echoed, coldness clutching at her, but then excitement began to throb in her breast and she drew a deep breath and met his steady gaze, aware that he expected her to cry off going.

'There's nothing to be scared about,' he retorted. 'I'm just about the best sailor on the island, no matter what Pete Blaine might have told you last evening.'

'Pete Blaine?' Jenny frowned. 'How did you know I was with him? And what's he got to do with it?'

'You can't do anything on this island without someone noticing and talking about it.' He smiled harshly. 'Now, sit down and keep out of my way until we're on the open sea.' He paused and considered for a moment. 'Perhaps you'd better go below into the main cabin until we're through the reef. I'd hate to lose you overboard in that rough water. By the way, are you a good sailor?'

'I'll let you know later,' Jenny

retorted determinedly, inwardly fighting against the mingled fear and excitement which filled her at the prospect of facing the reef with him.

4

When they were ready to leave the little harbour, Jenny allowed Craig to usher her below into the spacious main cabin, and she was surprised by the standard of luxury presented in the furnishings.

'When the boat begins to pitch you'd do well to lie on a bunk and lash yourself down,' he said. 'It won't be too bad, mind you, but if you haven't got good sea legs you might get thrown around a bit, and we don't want any injuries, do we?'

'I think I'd rather be on deck,' she decided. 'I do like to see what's going on.'

He nodded approvingly and led the way back into the stern cockpit. Jenny watched him cast off, and then he came back and started the engine. The boat surged forward, under the powerful thrust of its propellors, and they began to carve a furrow across the smooth waters of the bay. Jenny gazed ahead and was filled with sudden trepidation when she saw thundering surf on the reef in the distance. The gap looked impassable, but she realised that Craig would have done this many times, content to trust his judgement. Presently the vessel heeled over slightly, and she drew a deep breath and tensed herself for what she imagined would be a grim ordeal.

As they sped towards the reef, the smooth surface of the bay began to lift into tiny waves that gradually grew larger as they progressed. The roar of the powerful, marine engine muffled the noise of the heavy waves pounding on the reef, and Jenny felt as if she were watching a film on a cinema screen, except that the atmosphere grew tense as the boat began to defer to the grip of the sea.

She stood at his shoulder, her eyes narrowed against the glare. Masses of white water lay ahead, but she saw that they were making for a narrow strip of less-rough water that marked the exact passage through the reef, and very soon they were in the grip of the powerful currents surging through the gap.

Craig gave the engine more throttle and the boat shuddered as raw power surged through every plate and rivet. Broken water began tumbling over jagged coral on either side as they thrust into the narrow channel.

Craig leaned towards Jenny and shouted into her ear. 'Grab hold of that stanchion and hang on for your life,' he advised.

Jenny did so, and as surf flew in the sunlight she caught a glimpse of a beautiful rainbow. Her heart seemed uplifted as they continued, and she felt exultant as they won the battle against the ocean. She saw that Craig was filled with concentration, spinning the wheel deftly a few degrees to the left or to the right, and the steady power of the engine ensured that his slightest command was obeyed instantly.

Her heart swelled with emotion. She breathed deeply, filled with satisfying pleasure. Craig, she realised, had made no idle boast about the high degree of his seamanship.

Very soon, they entered a deeper channel and the broiling surf dropped behind. Great waves came at them with the speed of an express train, but the boat breasted them easily. Jenny began to breathe a little easier, and Craig smiled as he caught her eye. For the very first time in her life, Jenny felt vibrantly alive, and it was a sensation she did not wish to lose or forget.

When they reached the open sea there was hardly any motion of the surface, and it was like heaven after the tumult of the reef passage. Craig invited Jenny to take the wheel and she did so nervously, but he stood at her side, their arms touching while he gave her simple instructions. His nearness sent a tingle through her receptive body, and as the boat sped across the bright sea Jenny felt some of its power being transmitted

71

through her tense hands on the wheel.

'You'll make a good sailor,' Craig commented, and elation showed in her blue eyes as she glanced up at him. 'I'm going below, now, to make some coffee. You carry on.'

'What should I do if something goes wrong?' she demanded, scared by the thought of being left alone.

He laughed vibrantly. 'Nothing can go wrong, I assure you, but if the improbable happens, then I'd be here on the deck before you noticed that anything was amiss.'

'And if I see a craft coming from the opposite direction?'

'Steer round it!' His dark eyes were glinting in the sunlight, and there was a smile on his face which suited him. Jenny felt her heartbeats quicken as he chuckled. 'Don't worry,' he said lightly. 'I'm only joking! If you have any doubts about anything at all, just give me a shout. I'll hear you and come running.'

'All right!' She spoke doubtfully, and

he lifted a hand and clapped her lightly on the shoulder. She trembled at the contact but he did not seem to notice, and when he turned away and left the cockpit, Jenny drew a deep breath and suppressed a tiny shiver. She felt weak and shaken, and trembled as she steered the boat. There was a feeling deep inside her that warned of changes approaching, and she was surprised by the knowledge that she was impatient to face the future . . .

By the time Panaga appeared on the horizon, she had gained confidence in handling the boat. Craig looked out of the cabin a couple of times to see how she was making out, and then he left her to it. Then, as they drew nearer to the island, he appeared at her side and took over the wheel. Jenny stood relaxed at his side, gazing eagerly at the island they were fast approaching.

'We're running into a cove I own,' he said. 'In a few moments you'll see my house on the cliff above. It's a beautiful spot.' His tone changed then, she noticed, and he added, 'I've been thinking about selling out and going back to England, recently.'

'Are you?' Jenny could not keep concern out of her tone.

'Nothing is definite yet,' he said, gazing ahead, a distant expression in his eyes. He changed course slightly. 'No doubt you've been told about my recent history, and you must have gathered from the way I behaved on Taminga that I haven't recovered from the past yet.' He shook his head. 'There are too many bad memories around here for me. That's why I'm thinking of quitting.'

'There was cold weather in London when I left a few days ago.' Jenny suppressed a shiver at the memory. 'I wouldn't want to go back there after sampling this life.'

'You've only been out here a couple of days! Wait until the novelty wears off! You may have different ideas after a year or so.' He studied her face for a moment, and there was a seriousness in his eyes that made Jenny feel uneasy.

'But you're a nurse by profession, aren't you? I was forgetting that. I've always envied people in nursing. They have an all-consuming mission in life which overrides all other consider-ations. Their work exalts them. And I can see that quality in you.'

Jenny shook her head. She was beginning to realise that in his company her emotions became heightened. His personality was powerful enough to swamp her own impressions, and she could imagine that, given the chance to get to know him really well, she would probably fall head over heels in love with him. The knowledge filled her with anticipation.

They entered a narrow cove and the boat nosed in to touch a stone quay. Craig sprang ashore and tied up, then turned with a smile to hold out a hand for Jenny. She jumped ashore, but her foot slipped on treacherous stone and she fell against him, feeling his hard body, the powerful muscles of his chest as he grasped her instinctively, and for a moment she had the impression that he was going to embrace her, but he set her firmly on her feet and took hold of her elbow with strong but surprisingly gentle fingers, his face holding a half-smile.

'Mind the steps!' he warned, pointing to the rough-hewn ascent that led to the top of the cliffs. 'I slithered down from the top a couple of years ago.'

'You might have been killed!' she gasped.

'That wouldn't have worried anyone,' he retorted.

Jenny was breathless when they reached the cliff top, and Craig was breathing hard. They paused, and she looked around eagerly. There was the outline of a roof among the trees to the right, and she guessed his house was hidden there. Inland, the ground sloped away into rectangular fields, some of them overgrown and uncultivated, and an air of desolation struck through Jenny's heart. He had been letting things slide! He must have loved his wife deeply, despite the way she treated him! And it was a tragedy that such a man could not overcome his problems.

'Let's get on to the house,' he said, interrupting her thoughts, and took her arm again. Jenny walked silently by his side, prey to strange emotions. No man had ever affected her like this and she did not quite know how to handle the resulting emotions! She watched him covertly as they walked along a path that led through the heart of a grove, and he seemed to be lost in thought as he gazed ahead, his jawline set, apparently reliving some bad memories.

Presently, they emerged from the trees and came upon a house standing on a knoll, overlooking the cliff. The walls were pink-washed but the colour had faded, and the dark roof revealed the advances of Nature in the small clumps of grass growing among its tiles. There was a wonderful view of the cove from the terrace in front, and Jenny gazed down at Craig's boat where it lay like a boy's model in the bright sunlight.

'This is a fantastic view,' she observed. 'I've never seen anything quite like it.'

'Do you think so?' He shook his head as if mentally disagreeing. 'I used to like it here, but I got rid of all that nonsense a long time ago.'

'I'm sorry to hear that!' She tried to keep her tone light and casual. 'A life needs appreciation in it to be endurable.'

'That's true.' For a moment there was a smile on his lips, and his eyes were appreciative as he glanced at her. He nodded approvingly. 'You talk very sensibly,' he added.

'For a woman?' she countered, and his smile widened.

'Is it so obvious that my opinion of women is low?'

'I get the impression quite clearly, but not all women are alike.'

He shrugged. 'I realise that I've been in need of a reminder of that little lesson for quite some time now.'

'Your awareness proves that you're teaching yourself the lesson.'

'But it's more difficult that way, and takes much longer to accept.' He laughed and shook his head as he looked towards the house. 'Here comes Tilda, my housekeeper here.'

Jenny turned towards the house in some surprise, having thought that they were alone here, and saw an oldish woman of immense girth coming out to greet them. A heavy arm, the colour of old mahogany, was lifted to shield the woman's dark eyes, and a gaily-coloured turban covered a mass of tightly-crinkled hair. The black face was wrinkled and wise-looking and the wide mouth was stretched in a massive smile. As she approached, with ungainly gait, her eyes were expressing great pleasure.

'Master Craig!' she exclaimed. 'My Lordy! I never expected to see you on Panaga again. You've been away so long, I surely thought you'd kept your word to go back to England.'

'Not yet, Tilda! There were many times when I was tempted to flee, and truth to tell, it could come to that yet.'

'It would be the worst day's work you ever did!' The woman was studying Jenny intently while she spoke.

Jenny liked her instinctively. She had a soothing quality in her manner, and her brown eyes, glittering in the sunlight like a bird's, held hypnotic power in their depths.

'Tilda, this is Jenny. She's Tim Carr's sister, and she's just come to live on the island. She's going to work at the hospital there.'

'I'm pleased to meet you, Miss Jenny,' Tilda said pleasantly, and there was an intense sparkle in her gaze. 'I've been waiting a real long time to set eyes on you. There have been signs that you were coming.'

'You didn't know Tim Carr had a sister!' Craig scoffed with a grin. 'So don't try to mystify Jenny, Tilda.'

'I didn't know her as Jenny Carr,' the woman replied pridefully. 'But I sure enough knew she was coming.' She gazed at Jenny with unblinking eyes. 'And she's exactly as it was foretold,' she added.

'Don't start talking that kind of stuff,' Craig said, his expression suddenly harsh. 'You know I don't like it.'

'What kind of stuff is that?' Jenny demanded curiously.

'Never mind!' His face was grim, and he was looking at Tilda with a stern gaze. 'I forbid it, Tilda, and don't forget it.'

'Nothing on the subject will pass my lips.' The housekeeper smiled. 'I don't have to say anything.' She held Jenny's gaze, nodding slowly as if agreeing with the thoughts teeming in her mind. 'I hope you'll like living in the islands, Miss Jenny,' she said in a silky tone. 'I'm sure you do, but it will take you some time to make up your mind.'

'I do like it here,' Jenny replied quickly. 'I only wish I had been able to come years ago.'

'Yes. It's a pity you didn't, from many

points of view.' Tilda nodded emphatically. 'And I guess that's obvious to everyone now. Would you like a nice, cold drink, Miss Jenny? You're looking quite hot and bothered. You've been out in the sun far too long today, so you'd better come into the house and rest.'

She glanced contemptuously at Craig. 'If you don't care about yourself, Master Craig, then you should have more thought for your guest. Can't you see she ain't halfway 'climatised yet? And what about food? Why didn't you warn me you was coming? If you gave me prior notice of your coming, I'd have had something really nice ready for you.'

'Don't tell me you didn't know!' Craig responded with a grin. 'I heard Aya talking to you on the telephone before I left Taminga! So I expect you've performed your usual wonders in the kitchen. I have some business to attend to so I'm going to leave Jenny here with you until I get back. As you say, she's had enough sun for one day.'

He took hold of Jenny's arm again

and they went on to the house where Tilda led the way to an open veranda overlooking the sea. Jenny sank down upon a lounger with a sigh of relief, thankful for the slight breeze that was blowing in off the sea.

'I'll be quite happy to just sit and enjoy this view,' she said thankfully, aware that she was extraordinarily tired.

'I won't be long,' Craig said, his tone betraying that he was suddenly impatient to be on his way. 'Tilda will keep an eye on you, and just let her know if there's anything you want.'

'How's your head?' Jenny countered. 'You know you should have gone to hospital for a check-up.'

'I'm all right. It was only my head,' he retorted, and departed.

Jenny drew a deep breath as emotion filled her, and found it difficult to relax in her seat as she gazed out at the brilliant sea.

Tilda appeared, moving quite fast for someone of her immense bulk. She was carrying a tray containing a jug of cold lemonade which she set down on a small side table.

'Do you like this house, Miss Jenny?' she asked, breathing heavily from her ascent of the stairs. Her brown eyes had a piercing quality that seemed to bore through to Jenny's innermost thoughts.

'I like it very much, and could live here quite happily,' Jenny replied. 'I don't think I would ever tire of this view. Do you stay here alone, Tilda?'

'No. My husband takes care of this estate, although there is very little work being done at the moment. Perhaps Master Craig will change his mind now, about selling up and going to England. It would be a disaster if he left the islands.'

Craig returned later, by which time Jenny was feeling the atmosphere of the house very keenly. To her surprise he seemed to be in high spirits, and she wanted to ask him how his business had developed.

'Hello,' he greeted her, dropping on to the lounger at her side, and she

caught her breath at the unexpected-
ness of his action. He was very close,
and she felt an immediate response in
her mind. Her breathing quickened and
her pulses seemed to race. 'I hope
you're hungry after this morning's
excursion. Tilda has prepared a marvellous meal, and we'll have to do it justice
before she'll let us escape her clutches.
Has she looked after you?'

'Indeed she has.' Jenny smiled. 'And
how did your business go?'

'Quite well.' He nodded slowly, a
glint shining in his eyes. 'I've decided
not to sell just yet. I've had second
thoughts, and when in doubt, you
know!' He paused, then asked, 'Do you
like this place? How does it strike you?
You're a newcomer and I'd like to know
your first impressions.'

'I think everything about it is
marvellous! Just look at the view from
here.'

'It's rather frightening when there's a
storm.' He shrugged. 'But it's a sight
that shouldn't be missed. The waves

race across the cove and smash against the cliffs. Can you believe that the spray almost reaches the house here, which is over one hundred feet above sea level?'

'I'd like to see that. There's nothing more thrilling than an angry sea, if one is safe on dry land.' Jenny's eyes twinkled.

'Perhaps I can arrange it for you some day!' He smiled indulgently. 'But now it is time to eat. And we don't have to hurry back to Taminga, do we? I'd like to show you my secret place, where orchids grow like daisies.'

'Orchids!' she echoed, greatly interested.

'Do you like orchids?'

'They're my favourite flower! Our home in England was named Orchid House for me!'

'Then you're due for a surprise!' He seemed happy at her eagerness. Then, a frown crossed his face. 'That's if you can ride. There's no access for a car, and it's too far to walk.'

86

'I pride myself on my riding ability,' she responded.

'Great!' He smiled. 'This gets better and better. Let's have lunch now and we can set out for the orchids immediately after.'

They had a wonderful lunch, and Jenny afterwards praised Tilda, her words bringing a glitter of appreciation to the housekeeper's bright eyes. Then she and Craig set out on horseback for the secret place, and Jenny felt rather like a child again, off on some long forgotten school treat, past emotions returning as clearly as if they had never drifted away on the tides of the past.

The afternoon was perfect. There was no breeze and heat bore down upon them as they followed a narrow path across the fields. They were making for a line of hills rising up in the background, and cantered steadily side by side, with Craig pointing out the more memorable sights around them. When they reached a creek, Craig called a halt and they dismounted to let the horses drink. He gazed at Jenny across the back of his horse.

'Are you looking forward to nursing on Taminga?' he enquired.

'I am rather! I've always wanted to be a nurse, and I hate this business of being between jobs. It's so unsettling.'

'I know what you mean. It isn't a pleasant situation.'

Jenny nodded as she looked into his craggy face. 'But I made my decision in England to come out here for a fresh start and I have to be patient until the changes have taken place. It's difficult to stand at a crossroads in life, knowing a far-reaching decision may turn out to be wrong.'

'You've got it exactly.' There was sudden respect in his gaze, and he nodded slowly. 'It's exactly like standing at a crossroads! But you seem to have made the right decision, and I wish I could find it as easy.'

'It wasn't easy,' she said firmly, 'and it will be a long time before I'll know whether it was right or wrong.'

He gazed at her, and the silence that enveloped them seemed laden with significance.

'No,' he agreed. 'I don't suppose it was easy.' He looked away, and Jenny took the opportunity to study his profile. His brows were indrawn, his jaw set, and when he continued his tone sounded as if his thoughts were not behind his words. 'Nothing is easy in this world. At the time of my trouble it felt as if the end of the world had come. I just didn't care any more. Everything had finished, including my interest in life.' He looked at her and smiled. 'That's a long way down from which to start climbing up again, isn't it?'

'It is,' she agreed. 'But not impossible if you want to get back up.'

'I do want to!' There was a sudden edge to his voice, and she heard his sharp intake of breath. 'And I took a big step in the right direction today. I got rid of all thoughts of giving up and running back to England like a sick dog.' He smiled. 'Perhaps it was that bump on the head I got that changed my outlook!'

'Very probably, but that's the kind of therapy I wouldn't recommend to everyone,' Jenny countered.

They rode on to a small clearing and Craig dismounted, smiling at Jenny. 'This is where we leave the horses,' he confided. 'But it isn't far now.'

They continued on foot, pushing through tall ferns of every shade of green, and slender trees rose above them as if intent upon hemming them in for ever.

Presently, Jenny heard the musical sound of running water, but she could not see anything beyond the trees. It was as if Nature was jealous of human eyes discovering her beauty, and Jenny was eager to discover the spot which had captured Craig's heart. Then the trees thinned out and a wider clearing showed ahead. Jenny paused to look around, her heart filled with pleasure.

A torrent of water was cascading down a series of steep rocks in the hillside to form a waterfall, but Jenny's attention was quickly attracted by the masses of wild flowers that were growing uncultivated, and she uttered a cry of delight when she saw they were orchids.

'What did I tell you?' he demanded gently. 'Well, was it worth the effort to get here?'

'It's wonderful!' she gasped. 'Out of this world! I've never seen anything quite like it.' She spoke in a whisper, overawed by the beauty around her and filled with a tremoring emotion that defied her efforts to control it. She went forward and dropped to her knees in the lush green grass, putting her fingers to a fragile bloom that seemed wrought from porcelain. Orchids had always been her favourite flower, and she had never imagined them growing like this.

Craig came and kneeled at her side, selecting a bloom and plucking it carefully. He fixed it into her hair, intent upon what he was doing, and Jenny looked up into his intent face, shivering at their contact. Her skin seemed to burn where his fingers touched it.

'There, that sets you off,' he commented, leaning back on his heels and gazing at her with a smile of satisfaction on his lips.

Jenny gulped. She was unable to take her eyes off his face. He seemed to be gripped by the same unearthly emotion that held her, for there was a taut expression on his face and a glitter in his dark eyes. Then he smiled and leaned forward to kiss her lightly on the lips, and before it could register in her mind, he had got to his feet and backed away.

'Merely a salute to your beauty,' he said, his smile breaking the tension that enveloped them.

'And accepted in the spirit in which it was given,' she responded with a smile. Outwardly calm, her smile was frozen on her lips, and his action had left her weak and shaken. Her lips were on fire, her mind in turmoil, exalted by the beauty and wonder of her surroundings. The sound of the waterfall was insistent in her ears, and reality seemed far away.

5

When they started back to the house on the cliff, Jenny felt as if she were in a dream. Her mind was a jumble of impressions of Craig, and she studied him as they rode together. She looked at his eyes, his hair, the angles of his rugged face, and his features settled into her mind as if they had always belonged. There was no awkwardness, no diffidence between them. In fact, as time passed, Craig seemed to unwind. His manner became more open, his tone friendlier and less reserved. Gone was the aggressive manner he had used earlier. Now they were on relaxed terms. They used first names, and by the time they left the island and started the return trip to Taminga, Jenny could hardly remember what life had been like before she met him.

'Getting tired?' Craig's voice cut

across her thoughts.

'I am rather,' she admitted. 'It's been quite a hectic day, and I'm not fully acclimatised yet!'

'Well, you look as if this part of the world agrees with you.'

'And you seem to have taken a change for the better,' she said boldly.

'That's your influence!' He smiled. 'I must admit your company today has helped a great deal. I've already decided to stick it out here, and that's a good sign because I've been on the point of quitting and running for some time, although I've never been a quitter, but now I'm determined to climb back from the depths. It's all thanks to you, Jenny, and I'd like to spend some more time in your company, if you wouldn't mind.'

'I have a month's holiday before I report to the hospital,' she said, her pulses racing. 'So it will have to be now or never.'

He chuckled, and she saw brightness in his gaze. 'Then let's make a few plans, shall we?' he suggested. 'Or do you need to check with Debbie first?'

'Not really! Tim is busy every day, and Debbie has to be at home for Selina. No, I'm a free agent. But you may get bored with my company.'

He smiled. 'If I do, you'll be the first to know,' he countered. Then he sobered. 'And what about Peter Blaine?'

'What about him?' She watched his face for expression, wishing she knew exactly what was running through his mind.

'You were out with him.' Craig shrugged casually, as if he was not really concerned. 'He didn't waste much time making contact with you.'

'It was just the way that worked out,' she explained, frowning. 'Tim asked him to look me up when I arrived in Kingston. He happened to be there the same night, and Tim was concerned about me.' She suppressed a sigh. 'And to tell you the truth, I don't want to go out with him again.'

'Is that a fact?' He was surprised, but

seemed to like the idea.

Jenny nodded. 'There was something about him that repelled me,' she confessed. 'He seemed too intense at times, going over the top trying to impress me with what he has and what he hopes to do.'

'That sounds exactly like him!' The harsh tone remained in Craig's voice. 'I never got along with him!' He shook his head slowly. 'Still, it's not for me to talk about him. There was some mention that he might have had something to do with Ann's death!'

'Did you actually hear that?' she asked.

'Not in so many words. But there's nothing much can happen in the islands without someone learning about it. So I heard the rumours, and there was a time when I watched Blaine's movements, but it's not possible to prove anything after the event.

'Can you skin dive?' he enquired, changing the subject. She shook her head.

'Well, if you think the scenery on the island is wonderful then you've got to go underwater to round off your education.'

'Is it easy to do?'

'You'll soon find out.' His eyes glinted. 'I'm going to teach you.'

Jenny smiled. Looking ahead, she could see Taminga looming on the horizon, and experienced a pang of disappointment that the trip was almost over. Moistening her lips, she drew a deep breath. 'Before we get in,' she said quietly, making an effort to keep her tone neutral. 'I want to thank you for this fantastic day, Craig.'

'I'm the one who should be thanking you,' he protested, glancing at her with wrinkled brow.

'You asked me out in the first place — or should I say forced me?' Her eyes twinkled as she met his gaze.

'I suppose I was a bit forceful,' he admitted with a grin. 'Unfortunately, I got into the habit of being aggressive towards everyone. I suppose it was my only defence after what happened. And I certainly wasn't thinking straight at the time. It must have been that bump on the head.'

She laughed, and watched him as he concentrated upon navigating the boat. Every line of his face was etched in her mind now, and when she closed her eyes she could see the details clearly.

They chatted until they reached Taminga, and Jenny fell silent as they approached the passage through the reef. She had been nervous that morning, coming out, but the great waves seemed even more fearsome from behind.

Craig's skill at the wheel kept them away from the sharp coral that was waiting to rip the hull, and watching him intently, Jenny was well aware that her life lay in his hands.

They passed safely through the reef, and she began to breathe more easily again. Gradually, they found calmer water, and minutes later the boat nosed against the jetty, where Craig leaped ashore to tie up. Jenny uttered a great sigh as she stepped on to firm ground, and realised, too late, that her legs needed time in which to adjust. She staggered as the jetty seemed to rise and fall, but Craig was ready, and caught her before she lost her balance.

'I was expecting that,' he said, supporting her in his strong arms, and as she sagged against him, caught up in a paroxysm of undefinable emotion, he bent his head and casually kissed the tip of her nose. 'It will take you some time to find your sea legs,' he continued. 'But you're doing all right.'

'Do you think I'll ever be able to go through the reef without feeling that my last moments have come?' she asked as he released her. She was breathing deeply, fighting an impulse to thrust herself back into his embrace, and tiny tingles of pleasure were trickling through her breast.

'There's nothing to worry about so long as you're with me,' he said with a smile. He turned and glanced across the bay, but night was closing in quickly, and although they could hear the ceaseless roar of the waves they could hardly see the fearsome turmoil.

'It's been a wonderful day!' she declared with a trace of wistfulness.

'There can be as many more times like today as you wish,' he replied, taking hold of her arm.

'I shan't feel like starting work at the hospital if I continue to enjoy myself like this,' she protested.

'That proves you're not accustomed to having a good time, which is a pity. I'll have to find more activities to interest you.

'What about tomorrow?' Craig asked, helping her into his car.

'Anything you say.' She liked the way her heart was beating faster as she watched him walk around the vehicle to get into his seat.

'Do you have to go home now?' He seemed reluctant for the day to end, and Jenny was tempted to prolong her pleasure. At the moment it was in her to agree to anything he said, but she was exhausted, and dared not let the magic of the islands upset her sense of perspective.

'I think I do have to go home now,' she said softly. 'I'm so tired. It has been truly wonderful, but, now, I think I should go.'

He nodded understandingly and drove to Tim's bungalow. 'Here you are, safe and sound,' he said as he halted the car.

Tim appeared as they entered the bungalow, and greeted them cheerfully, although he studied Craig with an incisive gaze.

'Hello, so you've decided to return,' he observed. 'I was beginning to think you couldn't turn the boat around, Craig.'

'I never thought of that!' Craig countered. 'Perhaps the next time, eh?' He winked at Jenny.

Jenny was feeling incredibly tired. Her face felt as if it had received too much attention from the sun, and she was sure her hair was untidy. But she was contented for the first time in her life, and felt completely relaxed.

'Come and have a drink,' Tim said. 'I watched you coming through the reef. I don't know anyone who does it so easily, Craig. How did you get on at Panaga?'

Craig shrugged. 'I didn't sell out! I had changed my mind by the time I reached there. And I've made one or two other decisions as well! We're going into full production again. But we'll talk about that in the morning. Things are due to change. Tim, and you must be relieved to hear that,'

'It's very good news,' Tim agreed. 'And I'm pleased for your sake, Craig.'

Debbie appeared in the doorway, took one look at Jenny, and hurried to her side. 'You look exhausted,' she chided, and a sharp expression came to her face when she looked at Craig. 'What on earth are you thinking about?' she demanded. 'Jenny hasn't been on the island long enough to get accustomed to the climate, and she looks as if you've kept her out in the sun all day! Come and have a bath, Jenny. Then you must go to bed. You'll be lucky if you can get up in the morning.'

'And I must be going.' Craig caught Jenny's gaze. 'I'll call for you tomorrow about ten. I've a surprise in store for you so be ready and able to go out. Good-night now. Sleep well.'

'Good-night,' Jenny responded, experiencing a pang of disappointment as Debbie led her from the room and out of Craig's company.

'I've never seen Craig like this before,' Debbie said as they reached the bathroom. 'Whatever you've done to him, Jenny, it's a big change for the better. He's looking and acting as he was before Ann died.' She began to run the bath, her face intent. 'It looks as if you've brought him back to life, and that's a big responsibility because he'll come to depend on you, and if you ever turn your back on him he'll be finished! You do know that, don't you?'

'Well, isn't that a good thing? Look

how he's planning to get back to work. I expect that decision will make Tim's life easier at a stroke, and it must remove a great deal of worry from your shoulders.'

'That's true. But what about you? Craig can take care of himself, but you're just a girl. You had a bad time in England, and I wouldn't want to see you suffer again. Coming out here was supposed to make your life better.'

'Well I'm sure Craig would never knowingly hurt me!' Jenny said thoughtfully. 'He seems such a nice person, and I'd do anything to help him.'

'And what if there is any truth in the rumour that he knows something about Ann's death?' Debbie shook her head as she tested the water in the bath. 'By the way, Peter Blaine telephoned. He asked for you, and when I told him you were out he said he'd seen you leaving in the boat with Craig. That just proves you can't do anything on this island without somebody finding out about it. And he was most insistent that I warn you against Craig!'

'I think I can handle Craig,' Jenny said softly. 'And I can do him more good than harm, which is the only thing that concerns me at this moment. It's obvious that he needs help to get back on his feet, and if he thinks I can supply that help then he won't have to ask twice.'

'That's your professional instinct at work,' Debbie observed. 'But you won't be able to handle him as if he were a patient. Before you know it you'll become involved with him, which will place your whole future in his hands.'

'That's possible.' Jenny nodded. 'But I feel I'm doing the right thing, and that's all that matters. I'm a great believer in intutition.'

'I'm only thinking of you!' Debbie said quietly. 'But go ahead and do what you think you should. I just hope you're right.'

'And so do I,' Jenny added.

* * *

The ensuing days were blissful. Craig called for Jenny each morning, intent upon showing her around the island and introducing her to its way of life. She spent many sunny hours in his company, and each passing day found her life becoming just a little more closely entwined with his. She did not question her feelings because the emotions filling her were so exquisite she could not bear to analyse them. And the changes in Craig were all too evident. He was beginning to smile and the knowledge that it was good for him made her feel even more disposed towards him. By the end of her first week on Taminga, she was happy only when they were together . . .

Peter Blaine arrived at the bungalow one evening after she had returned home from a day out with Craig, and Jenny felt the first draught of chilling reality. Peter was grim-faced, and wasted no time getting to the point of his visit. Tim offered him a drink, but Peter shook his head.

'I'd like to talk to Jenny alone,' he said, staring at her across the room.

'I was on the point of going to help Debbie put Selina to bed.' Tim arose and walked to the door, pausing to glance at Jenny, who smiled at him reassuringly as he departed.

'Won't you sit down?' Jenny invited.

Blaine crossed the room to stand before her, and she was surprised to sense menace in every line of his tense body.

'I've been telephoning every day to talk to you,' he said reprovingly, 'and you're always out with Hannant! Can't you see you're wasting your time with him? He's nothing more than a beach-comber these days! And he's not the type of man you should associate with if you hope to live decently on the island.'

'Really!' Jenny was ready to spring to Craig's defence. 'You have no right to come here talking like that, I have no wish to listen.'

'Do you know that Hannant is living with a local girl?'

'Craig's life is his own business,' she countered.

'You don't believe me? Well I can produce the girl, if you need proof. I can't believe you would condone that way of life.'

'It's none of my business!' Jenny said sharply. 'And I certainly don't need you to teach me morals. What business is it of yours, anyway?'

'I'm trying to prevent you making a complete fool of yourself. People are talking about you keeping company with Hannant, and I wanted to introduce you to my circle of life on the island, but you're making things diffi-cult. Nobody socialises with Craig Hannant these days!'

'I'm sorry about that, but I have always chosen my own friends, and I won't change my habits for you or anyone else. Perhaps you'd better leave. I don't like the way you seem to have taken it upon yourself to interfere in my life.'

'You could be very sorry for taking this attitude,' he warned. 'If you care nothing for yourself then have some thought for your brother. Tim has to live and mix with these people.'

Debbie walked into the room and paused. 'I must ask you to keep your voice down, Peter,' she said coldly. 'I've just put Selina to bed.'

'If you'll excuse me, I have to wash my hair,' Jenny cut in. 'And perhaps it would be as well if you didn't come to see me again.'

Blaine glared at her, his dark eyes seeming to smoulder, and then he sighed and shook his head. 'My only concern is to save you a lot of grief,' he said. 'But if you can't be told, then you'll just have to make the best of it.' He nodded curtly and turned on his heel to depart.

Jenny sighed as the engine of his car roared out, and when silence returned she let her shoulders slump.

'I've been expecting something like this to develop,' Debbie observed.

'Peter is a very forceful man. I don't know what he has in mind, but he could make a lot of trouble for everyone.'

'Do you think I ought to stay away from Craig, too?' Jenny asked.

'Heaven forbid! Don't get me wrong. I'm not trying to interfere. Just be careful, that's all. Craig is such an uncertain man. He was interested in a girl last year, and for a few weeks he seemed a changed man. But she left the island and he soon returned to his old ways.'

Jenny was thoughtful, her head filled with Blaine's hurtful words. Was Craig living with a local girl? Of course it was none of her business, but she was perturbed by the thought, and went to bed that night full of uncertainty. Yet she was certain of one thing. She would have nothing more to do with Peter Blaine.

For three days Jenny saw nothing of Blaine, and the sharpness of her memory began to fade, but the very

111

next morning, as Craig picked her up at the bungalow, Blaine's car arrived, totally blocking the narrow track to the road. Jenny felt her nerves tighten at the sight of his sharp, unsmiling face, and glanced quickly at Craig, who was looking at Peter with narrowed eyes.

Blaine alighted from his car and walked to where Jenny was seated in Craig's car. He ignored Craig, who was in the act of sliding into the driving seat, and paused at Jenny's open window, bending slightly to peer in at her.

'Hello,' he said, not quite able to sound really friendly, and there was a smile on his face, although it was not natural and looked forced. 'You're so difficult to catch at home these days I thought I'd call early in an attempt to see you — it certainly isn't possible to talk to you on the telephone!'

'That's because I'm on holiday,' Jenny said carefully. 'In two weeks I start working at the hospital.'

'And you're busy today!' He let his

gaze flicker to Craig, who was watching him intently, but neither spoke.

'I thought we settled the situation between us the other evening,' Jenny said in some desperation.

'You were tired then, so I didn't take any notice of what you said.' He had evidently dismissed her attitude out of hand. 'I'd like to invite you to my club again, but I won't embarrass you by asking for a date in front of Hannant. I'll telephone again one evening.' He stepped back and turned away, and Jenny exhaled deeply as he returned to his car and drove off.

Craig was grim-faced and silent as he drove along the track, while Jenny tried to make light of the situation, but she realised there really was bad blood between Craig and Blaine, and surmised that there had to be a very good reason for its existence.

'I don't like Blaine,' Craig said as he parked the car, and for a moment he sat gripping the steering wheel. 'The very sight of him rubs me up the wrong way!

And don't ask me why! There's never been any trouble between us. It's just one of those things, I suppose. And I can sense you don't like him, Jenny!'

'I certainly don't!' She was quite definite about that as they walked down to the beach, where Craig had a chalet under a cluster of palms, 'But he won't take no for an answer.'

'You went out with him that first evening and he now regards you as his property. He's like that, so I've heard. And he's no good, Jenny, If you want to go out with him then do so by all means! But be careful.'

'I don't want to go out with him again,' she said firmly.

'Then let's forget about him!' Craig's tone was surprisingly harsh. 'He could spoil my day, I can tell you!'

They went into the chalet and Jenny changed into her swim suit while Craig readied two sets of underwater equipment. He helped her into one set, and smiled as he looked into her eyes.

'Before we start just remember the

lessons I've given you. You're ready to take the plunge now. And don't forget I'll be close to you all the time so don't panic about anything. If you think something might be going wrong then just look at me for reaction.'

'I trust you, Craig,' she said softly. 'I'll be all right.'

'I liked the way you said that,' he commented. 'Now go down to the water's edge and I'll join you when I'm ready.'

Jenny nodded, and set off, carrying flippers in her hand. She sat down on the beach with her feet in the water, and there was such a feeling of happiness inside her that she felt almost unable to contain it. Putting on her flippers, she had difficulty getting to her feet, and Craig, on his way to her, came laughingly to her rescue.

'You look like a beached porpoise,' he commented, and leaned forward and kissed her lightly on the lips. 'That's for luck,' he added as she caught her breath. He seemed quite elated, and smiled as he took her hand. 'Come on, let's get into the water.'

Jenny nodded, fighting to cope with the emotions filling her. They entered the water, turned on their oxygen, and then slid easily beneath the surface. When she was swimming underwater she felt as free as a fish, and looked around with pleasure at what was a totally different world. There was complete silence, apart from the flow of bubbles from her air supply.

There was so much to see that Jenny could imagine her eyes were almost popping out behind her face mask. She kept looking at Craig, who remained within arm's length, and he waved and took her hand to lead her into deeper water. They went out farther from the shore, moving around like two catfish scavenging the bottom, and she looked around in child-like wonder, filled with great pleasure at what she saw.

When Craig attracted her attention and pointed upwards she wondered if something was wrong. They surfaced, and she was astounded when he said they had been down for the limit of their dive. They waded ashore and sat on the beach in the sun. Jenny felt marvellous, quite exhilarated by the experience of the morning, and proud of her new achievement.

Craig smiled indulgently as she chattered excitedly about what she had seen.

'We can go down every morning if you like it so much,' he said. 'That's no problem. But what are we to do with our afternoons? Today is well taken care of. We're going to my place for lunch, which has been arranged. And this afternoon I thought we'd take a look at an inland village before going to a fishing village on the other side of the island. How does that sound to you?'

'Ideal,' she responded, content to let him make their plans.

'Good. Come on, then. Let's get changed. We'll need plenty of time for this afternoon's excursions.'

When they reached the house, Jenny

was surprised to be served by Aya, the girl who cleaned house for Debbie, and she was shocked when she greeted the girl cheerfully only to be rebuffed by a surly manner. Recalling how friendly Aya had been when they met in Debbie's house, Jenny was confused by the change of attitude, until she recalled that Debbie had said Aya was in love with Craig, then she understood.

By the time Craig returned her to the bungalow, Jenny was tired but very happy. Craig switched off the engine and sat looking at her for a moment, until she settled down and became silent.

'You certainly know how to enjoy yourself when we're out,' he commented.

'And why not?' She laughed lightly. 'I've never had a holiday like this before.'

'That's because you didn't know me before,' he said, and she caught her breath and looked intently at him.

He nodded slowly, reaching out to

place his hands upon her shoulders, his gaze holding hers. Jenny felt a stab of excitement as she became aware of his intention, and made no move to stop him when he drew her into a close embrace. He held her tenderly and kissed her, as she closed her eyes and tried to relax. Pleasure filled her, and she responded instinctively, aware that their contact was the sweetest thing she had ever known. Time seemed to stand still, and the silent darkness encompassing them was warm and friendly.

Finally, Craig drew back, his eyes gleaming, a half-smile of satisfaction on his lips. 'I've been wanting to do that for some time,' he said. 'But now you'd better go in, Jenny. I'll call for you at ten in the morning. OK?'

'OK,' she said, speaking lightly with great difficulty, for her pulses were racing. 'See you tomorrow.'

6

'Hello,' Debbie greeted when Jenny walked into the lounge. 'I've been hoping you wouldn't be long. There's a message from Frank Carter. He'd like you to call him at the hospital as soon as possible.'

'What's wrong?' Jenny demanded.

'They have an epidemic of food poisoning. Some of the staff have gone sick and Frank is short of trained help, so he's hoping you can go in tomorrow and assist for a few days. Shall I get him on the phone for you?'

'Please! And I'll certainly help.' Jenny smiled as she spoke, but inside she was conscious of disappointment. She wouldn't be able to see Craig, as they had planned. She suppressed a sigh, and made the effort to control her emotions as Debbie picked up the telephone.

'I'm sorry about this, Jenny,' Frank Carter said when she spoke to him. 'But I'm at my wit's end, and I'd be grateful if you could give us a hand for a few days.'

'Of course,' she replied without hesitation. 'What time would you like me to report tomorrow?'

'Would eight be all right?'

'Certainly. I'll be there on the dot.'

'Thank you, and you'll be able to take the rest of your holiday when we get back to normal.'

'That's all right. It's no problem.' Jenny hung up and looked at Debbie, who was watching her. 'I'm going on duty at eight in the morning. Now I'll have to ring Craig. We had made arrangements for tomorrow.'

Jenny dialled the number, and a moment later a female voice answered.

'Aya,' she said. 'This is Jenny Carr. I'd like to speak to Craig, please.'

'He's very busy at the moment.'

Jenny frowned, recognising enmity in the girl's tone. And what was Aya

121

doing in Craig's home at this time of the evening?' The question rose unbidden in her mind and she drew a deep breath.'

'This is quite important,' she said. 'If Craig is in the house, then please tell him I'm calling.'

'Wait a moment.' Aya's tone was sharp, and there was a clatter as she put down the receiver.

'Hello?' Craig said at the other end of the telephone. 'Are you there, Jenny?'

'Hi, Craig,' she responded. 'I've got some bad news, I'm afraid.' She explained the situation and fell silent to hear his reaction.

'That's a pity,' he said. 'By the sound of it there's no way around it. You'll have to go and we must make the best of it. Still, it's only for a few days and that will soon pass. It might be a blessing in disguise, really. I do have a lot of work to get through and I can get to it instead of shelving it.'

'That sounds like a good idea!' she agreed quickly. 'I'm disappointed this has come up, but there's nothing else I can do.'

'All right. I'll pick you up at seven-thirty in the morning and drive you into town. That will give me a chance to see you. And I'll pick you up when you get off duty. Have you any idea when that will be?'

'No. I'll ring you as soon as I find out.'

'Let's leave it like that then. See you in the morning, Jenny.'

The next morning, when Craig called for her, Jenny studied him critically as he drove into town. He was unhappy about not seeing her during the day, and she wondered just how much he had come to rely upon her since they'd been together, for his disappointment seemed as great as hers!

'The days will soon pass,' she consoled when he threw a glance at her.

'Indeed! And I've got so much to do I hardly know where to start. I want to get things moving so when you're finished at the hospital again I'll be able to take some days off without too much of a guilty conscience.' He smiled. 'I just hope that when you do start nursing full-time, all these little jaunts and trips of ours will not become a thing of the past.'

'They won't if I have anything to do with it,' she said firmly. 'I shall get time off, you know. But I expect you'll be the one who's too busy. You have some new ideas you want to put into practice, and when you start you won't have time for anything so unimportant as taking me out.'

'Don't you believe it!' He drew in at the hospital gate and turned to take hold of her hands. 'Call me when you find out what time you'll be coming off duty.'

'Will you be at home all day?'

He nodded. 'Oh, yes. I'll be working around, but someone will take a message when you call.'

'Perhaps it's as well I am going to work,' she mused. 'This holiday has to end sometime and I have to get into the right frame of mind for work.'

He smiled, and Jenny felt reluctant to leave him. But she got out of the car, and paused to wave to him when she reached the hospital entrance. He was sitting motionless in the car, watching her, and she smiled encouragingly. He returned the wave, then drove away, and she went resolutely into the hospital, her mind filled with thoughts of him.

Jenny had no time to dwell upon her emotions when she reported for duty, for she was given a uniform and barely enough time in which to change. Frank Carter was apologetic as he showed her around, and Jenny steeled herself, pushing her disappointment into the background.

'Have you any idea when I might get off duty later?' she asked. 'I have to inform someone of my plans.'

'I have some extra help coming in around seven this evening. They're off-duty nurses, too,' he said. 'Could you hang on until then?'

'Yes, indeed!' Jenny nodded and went into a ward office to call Craig. But he had not reached home yet, and she left a message with Aya . . .

Time ceased to exist as Jenny set to work, for duty demanded all she had. There was an acute shortage of trained staff and her skills were very much in demand. It was as if she had boarded a merry-go-round, and confusion seemed to reign until she found her stride and did what she could to alleviate the situation.

At seven that evening, Frank Carter came to release her from duty, and Jenny was exhausted. Promising to return at eight the next morning, she left the hospital and stood by the gate, looking around expectantly for Craig. But there was no sign of him. There was a small park opposite the hospital gate, and she saw a telephone box nearby. Hurrying across the road, she called Craig's number, and was relieved when he answered immediately.

'Jenny!' His relief was obvious. 'You

promised to let me know when you'd get off duty.'

'But I called this morning as soon as I knew!' she protested. 'You hadn't returned home at that time so I left a message with Aya!'

'Aya! Come to think of it, I haven't set eyes on her all day! That girl! Just wait until I see her! Have you finished now?'

'Yes. I'm at the hospital gate waiting for you,' she responded.

'Give me twenty minutes!' he said.

'Wait!' she said anxiously. 'Listen, Craig. No reckless driving.'

'As if I would!' He chuckled. 'I'm on my way! I've been waiting for this moment all day!' The line went dead, and Jenny slowly replaced the receiver.

She found a seat in the park and sat down to wait, finding her thoughts over-active as she considered. She had missed Craig, and wondered how he had accepted the great change in his life. She was taking a deep interest in him, she was aware, and had become emotionally involved, sensing that she wanted the relationship to progress from there. Craig would regain his emotional balance as he recovered from the traumas of the past, she knew, and felt good about the new situation.

When Craig arrived, he leaped out of his car with a grin on his face and grasped her hands. Jenny felt all her doubts vanish into thin air at the sight of him and was thrilled when his narrowed eyes studied her. But a frown touched his face when he saw how tired she was.

'Hey! I'll bet you haven't stopped once all day! And I thought I was busy! You must be careful, Jenny. You're not used to this climate yet, and you should take things easy at first.'

'I'm all right,' she said softly. 'It's just that the first day back to nursing is always strenuous!' She walked with him to the car and he settled her in the front passenger seat, fussing unnecessarily to make her comfortable, and she loved every minute of it. 'I want to hear about your day,' she added. 'What have you been doing?'

'Perhaps you should ask Tim that question when I'm not around. Then you might get a true answer.' He smiled. 'I have the feeling I've done nothing but get in Tim's way today, and one thing I learned is how badly I let the business down. But we've stopped the rot, and there's only hard work between me and success.'

'That's good news!' Jenny stifled a yawn. 'Excuse me, but I am tired. It's been a long, long day!'

'I'll take you home,' he decided, helping her into the car. 'You'd better get some rest or you won't make it through tomorrow.'

'But I don't want to go home now,' she protested.

'You'd better do as you're told,' he countered gently. He drove through the town and Jenny relaxed in her seat, her head nodding.

When they reached the bungalow, Craig touched her shoulder, and Jenny realised she had been drowsing.

'Poor girl!' he said. 'You're practically out on your feet. And you've got it all to do again!'

'I'll be much better tomorrow,' she replied, 'if that's any consolation. Are you coming in?'

'No, as much as I'd like to.' He shook his head. 'You're too tired! I'll pick you up in the morning and drive you to the hospital. Same time?'

Jenny nodded, and he leaned across and kissed her lightly. She reached out and touched his face, and he pressed his lips to her fingers.

'Go in and get some rest,' he said firmly. 'We'll get together again when the hospital crisis is over.'

She left him and went into the bungalow, where Debbie took one look at her and uttered a cry of horror.

'I know,' Jenny said. 'Craig has been telling me what a wreck I look. But I'll be all right after a good night's sleep. I'll just take a shower and then tumble into bed.'

'Frank rang a few moments ago to ask how you were feeling,' Debbie said. 'And now I can understand why. Was it very busy at the hospital?'

'I've never been busier,' Jenny responded.

After showering, Jenny went to bed, but despite her tiredness she was unable to sleep immediately, and lay in the darkness for a long period, her thoughts busy. Everything had changed drastically overnight. The happiness she had experienced when Craig took her out to Panaga that first day was now only a happy memory, and she was concerned about what might have happened on the island before she arrived. Doubt began to rear its ugly head. Craig's dead wife was beginning to haunt her mind, raising the question of what had really happened to her.

Jenny turned restlessly and tried to relax, and by degrees her mind quietened and tiredness finally won the battle for her attention. She fell into a deep sleep and knew nothing more until sunrise, when she opened her eyes to the realisation that a day just like the previous one had dawned . . .

And so it proved to be. Craig drove her to the hospital and she spent endless hours at the beck and call of everyone who needed attention. The morning seemed to drag by, and there were innumerable problems to be solved, with many hectic incidents that demanded concentration and dedication. By the end of the day she was utterly exhausted, and Craig, when he picked her up, said nothing and took her straight home.

On the afternoon of the fourth day, two of the nurses who had been sick returned to duty, and for the first time since she donned her uniform, Jenny found time to think.

She was going to the canteen for coffee when a voice called her name and she looked round in surprise to see Peter Blaine coming along the corridor. He halted before her, his eyes narrowing as he took in her appearance.

'I hardly recognised you dressed like

that,' he said. 'But this is an improvement on the way you were spending your days, and I'd like you to have an evening out with me when you get the time. There are lots more places I want to show you.'

'You don't take no for an answer, do you?' she countered. 'I've made it quite plain that we have nothing in common, and it would be a waste of time and energy for us to get together again.'

'You'd do better for yourself by dropping Hannant and seeing me instead,' he retorted, his lips pulling into an uncompromising line. 'There isn't any future for you with him. Haven't you heard the rumours about him? He knows more about his wife's death than ever came out.'

'I'm not interested in gossip,' Jenny said impatiently. 'Now, if you'll excuse me, I must go.'

'You're not listening to me,' he rapped. 'And I'm warning you that only disaster can come from your association with Craig Hannant.'

Jenny walked away from him, her mind troubled by his warning, which kept repeating itself with maddening frequency. She was in love with Craig! The knowledge came out of the blue, and she accepted it as she went back to duty. Whatever had happened in the past, before her arrival on the island, she was now in love with Craig Hannant! Her mind proclaimed the fact, and her pulses hammered the message to every part of her body . . .

At seven o'clock that evening, when she went off duty, Jenny looked around eagerly for Craig's car and was surprised to find he had not arrived. She was immediately concerned, for he had made a habit of being there when she emerged from the hospital. She waited ten minutes before succumbing to impatience, and then hurried to the phone box on the corner. But a car drew up beside her, and, as she turned eagerly, her spirits sank when she found Peter Blaine peering at her.

Jenny turned away from him some-what angrily. What was wrong with him? Did he need the message spelled out in words of one syllable?

'Wait a minute, Jenny,' he called. 'I know where Hannant is.'

She halted in mid-stride and turned to face him as he got out of the car. His expression was grim, and his eyes were glinting as he halted before her.

'Well?' she demanded. 'Where is Craig?'

'In my office at the hotel. He's had too much to drink and is sleeping it off. But I knew he was supposed to be here to meet you, and I don't like the idea of you being treated like this. I've already told you Hannant isn't to be trusted, and perhaps now you'll believe me.' He looked at her smugly.

'Will you take me to him?' she asked.

'That's why I'm here. But I'm only doing it for you. I wouldn't cross the street to help him. Among other things, I didn't like the way he used to treat his wife.'

Jenny said nothing, and sat motionless beside him while he drove her to the hotel. Her mind was filled with foreboding as he led the way into his office, and she was shocked to see Craig stretched out senseless on a couch.

'How long has he been like this?' she demanded, going to Craig's side and examining him. She could smell whisky on him, and lifted an eyelid. Her lips tightened when she discovered that he was deeply unconscious.

'He was drinking in the hotel bar for a couple of hours,' Blaine told her, 'and when one of the barmen warned me that he'd had more than enough I had him brought in here out of harm's way.'

'Have you any idea where his car is?'

'In the hotel car park, at the rear.'

'Then perhaps you'll have him put in the car and I'll drive him home.'

Blaine looked at her, gauged the degree of her determination, and sighed as he nodded. Jenny fought down her tiredness and watched as two men carried Craig out the back door and put him in the waiting car. She thanked Blaine for his help and then quickly departed, driving Craig out to his home. Her thoughts were bleak during the trip, and she kept glancing at Craig, wondering how this could have happened.

When she drew up outside Craig's front door she saw Aya in the garden. The girl came quickly at the sound of the car, and Jenny saw her changing expression as they confronted each other.

'You must help me get Craig into the house,' Jenny said.

'What is wrong?' Aya demanded. 'What have you done to him?'

'Don't be silly! I've just come off duty at the hospital. He's had too much to drink, that's all. Help me get him into the house and then we'll bring him back to his senses.'

It was an effort to lift Craig's dead weight out of the car and into the house, but they managed it between them and deposited him on a sofa in the big lounge.

'Make some strong, black coffee,' Jenny instructed, and bent over Craig while Aya departed for the kitchen. Craig was still unconscious, and Jenny shook her head slowly. She had not expected this turn of events. He had seemed to be keen to get back to normal, had talked of new plans and fresh endeavours, but this was a bad setback, and she was both disappointed and sad.

When Aya returned with coffee she put down the tray and flounced out of the room again, but Jenny had no time for the girl's attitude. She endeavoured to get some coffee into Craig's system, shaking him and tugging at his shoulder until he stirred. Then she spoke sharply until his eyes flickered open.

'I want you to drink some coffee, Craig,' she commanded.

He shook his head and seemed to drift into unconsciousness again, but she persevered, and after several attempts he began to sip the coffee. Jenny kept at him, stopping him from

138

falling asleep again, and his awareness returned by degrees. By the time he had drunk two cups of coffee his eyes were open, and he stared rather blearily at her, shaking his head and frowning, as if he could not accept the situation.

'Jenny!' he managed to say at last. 'I was about to come and meet you! What are you doing here?' He blinked and glanced round. 'And how did I get here? I was in town, waiting to pick you up. Did I meet you at the hospital? Did I bring you back here?'

'You didn't,' she countered. 'I had to bring you home.'

'Bring me home?' He was frowning, evidently trying to recall events.

'You went into Blaine's hotel for a drink and took rather more than was good for you,' Jenny explained, and he pushed himself erect and stood swaying, staring at her in disbelief.

'I certainly didn't!' he retorted. 'I went in for a beer because I was thirsty, and I had only one.' He moistened his lips, his eyes narrowing as he tried to remember. 'Blaine was at the bar, and he offered me a tot from his special bottle. I didn't want to accept a drink from him, but I didn't want any trouble so I took it, and that's the last thing I can remember. I'm sure I didn't even finish the drink!'

'Are you suggesting that Blaine did this to you deliberately?' Jenny stared at him, unable to believe the thoughts entering her head.

'Well, you can believe that one drink wouldn't knock me out,' he retorted.

'I could smell whisky on your breath when I first saw you,' she said.

'I didn't take more than a sip from Blaine's drink. So what happened? I don't know right now, but I'm going to find out. And you really thought I'd drunk myself stupid?'

'What was I to think, when Blaine arrived at the hospital instead of you?'

'I'll have a few words with Blaine.' Craig's hands clenched. 'I don't know what's going on, but this is too much!

Why would he want to make it appear as if I'd been drinking heavily?' He swayed as he faced Jenny. 'I can see you don't believe me,' he said.

'I don't know what to think,' she responded.

'Well, have a chat with Tim. I was working with him all day, and I left myself with just enough time to get to town and meet you.'

'And Blaine arranged all this to discredit you in my eyes?' Jenny asked. 'Why on earth would he want to do that?'

'I'll be interested in his answer to that question when I can get around to putting it to him,' Craig said harshly. He looked closely at her, and the anger went out of him. 'How are you feeling this evening? You don't look so tired. Was it as bad today?'

'No, and two nurses who were sick came back on duty this afternoon.'

'Does that mean you don't have to go in tomorrow?'

Jenny shook her head. 'I'll have to go

in for two more days at least. But I'll be relieved when this little stint is over.'

He walked tentatively around the room, staggering a little, and then came back to Jenny for another cup of coffee.

'I feel as if I've been drugged,' he complained.

She nodded. 'That's my opinion, for what it's worth! But why would Peter Blaine do this to you?'

Craig shook his head as he considered, and Jenny sighed.

'I think you had better maintain a prudent distance between yourself and Blaine in future,' she suggested. 'And it wouldn't help to confront him because he would only deny any knowledge of such a preposterous action. But you can let the episode be a warning, Craig, and be on your guard in future.'

'Don't worry!' He placed his hands on her shoulders and looked into her face. 'I won't fall for any of his tricks again.'

The door opened behind them and Aya entered the room, pausing on the threshold when she saw them standing together.

'Do you need any more coffee?' she demanded.

'No, thank you,' Jenny replied, and waited until the girl had departed. 'If you're feeling well enough now I'd like to go home, she added. 'But if you're not up to driving then perhaps I can borrow your car.'

'I'll drive you,' he said. 'The coffee has killed whatever it was I drank in Blaine's place.' He looked into Jenny's eyes, saw the doubt and confusion that gripped her, and shook his head slowly. 'There's always been bad blood between Blaine and me,' he mused. 'I had to warn him away from my wife at one time. Now he has designs on you, and that's why this happened today. But he's gone as far as he can now, and after this there's no way he can win.'

7

When Craig dropped Jenny off at the bungalow, after promising to collect her early the next morning, she had decided to say nothing to Tim and Debbie about the strange incident involving him. However, when she saw them relaxing on the veranda she knew she had to tell them what had happened.

'You're later this evening,' Debbie said, getting to her feet. 'Would you like a drink? You're looking quite hot and bothered.'

'Thanks, I'd like something long and cold,' Jenny responded, sitting down.

'I'm sure they're working you too hard,' Tim observed. 'You must be careful, Jenny, or you'll be cracking up.'

'I'm fine,' she said. 'But something happened today and I wonder if you can throw any light on it.'

'What's the trouble, Sis?' Tim sat up a little straighter, his narrowed eyes regarding her intently. 'Has someone been bothering you?'

She explained what had happened to Craig and saw Tim's face tighten into harsh lines. He leaned sideways and placed a hand upon her arm.

'I've been afraid the past would suddenly burst into the open,' he said. 'It seemed to die naturally after Ann Hannant was buried, but it looks as if matters will have to come to a head before it can finally be settled.' He paused for a moment, evidently pondering over what he knew.

'You're talking in riddles, Tim,' she said.

'Sorry. Obviously, you know nothing of what happened on the island before your arrival. And I'm sorry I asked Peter to look out for you at Kingston when you arrived. If you hadn't met him then he wouldn't have decided he wanted to get to know you better. And of course we didn't suspect that Craig would get interested in you.'

'So what happened in the past?' Jenny demanded. She smiled and thanked Debbie for the drink which was handed to her.

'Let me say that Craig certainly didn't have time to drink himself silly in town today,' Tim said firmly. 'He was working with me all day. In fact it looked like he was going to be late. So if he says he had just one drink then he did.'

'I know Peter Blaine wanted to discredit Craig in my eyes,' Jenny replied. 'But this trouble between them goes much deeper than Blaine wanting to get to know me better, doesn't it? Surely it has to do with Craig's wife and the way she died.'

Tim nodded slowly. 'That's about it,' he admitted, 'although no-one knows exactly what happened. It's not even proved that Ann didn't die accidentally.'

'But there was a lot of talk,' Debbie cut in. 'And we all know there's no smoke without fire!'

'Is it likely that Craig killed his wife?' Jenny asked, looking into Tim's eyes,

'I heard that rumoured more than once, but I'd stake my life on Craig,' Tim replied. 'He did everything humanly possible to make that marriage work, but it was a losing battle. You can believe that, Jenny, because I was closest to Craig most of the time, and I saw things no-one else did.'

Jenny nodded. 'So what about the rumours of his wife's death?'

Tim shook his head, and there was a troubled expression in his eyes. 'That's all they were. Just rumours. Ann had got herself mixed up with a group dabbling in black magic and a local religion, but no-one knew anything for certain. And I really don't know how the rumours started.

'It was said that she didn't accidently drive over the cliff, that the car had been tampered with and she couldn't stop. Mind you, she had been drinking. Twice that I know of, she had to be lifted out of the car after she'd run into something, and each time she was practically insensible with drink.'

'So it's not surprising she ended up the way she did,' Jenny remarked. 'And all the talk about her being murdered is probably just talk?'

'I'm sure.' Tim sighed and shook his head. 'The police carried out the most exhaustive enquiries, which revealed nothing sinister. But the past is not what should interest us now, you know. Craig seems to be emerging from his black tunnel, and we ought to be doing all we can to help him. Aya is the only one who is thinking straight. She'd lay down her life for Craig, and in the past she's warned me several times when he's been heading for trouble, enabling me to extricate him. I think I'll have a word with her. She'll watch out for him.'

'She may not want to now I'm on the scene,' Jenny said softly, explaining the girl's changed attitude.

Tim shook his head. 'She'll do it for Craig,' he said confidently . . .

At the hospital next morning, there was a telephone call for her, and Jenny was surprised when she recognised Aya's voice.

'Your brother spoke to me about Craig and I would like to talk to you,' the girl said, her tone neutral.

'Fine,' Jenny agreed. 'When can we meet?'

'The sooner the better. I have things to tell you. Can you get away from the hospital at all?'

'I have a lunch break in about an hour. I usually eat in the canteen here, but I can leave the hospital.'

'I'll be outside the hospital gate at twelve-fifteen,' Aya decided. 'I won't take up much of your time.'

The line went dead, and Jenny frowned as she replaced the receiver. She could only wonder what Aya had to say, and fought down her impatience as she returned to the ward. She was kept very busy, but time seemed to drag until she went off duty and saw Aya waiting outside.

'I'm here to try and help, because Tim asked me to come,' Aya said as they sat down on a seat in the small park opposite the hospital. 'I saw last evening how much you helped Craig. So we are on the same side of the fence. I would do anything for Craig, and he is in trouble, although he can't see it. I have told him certain things which he does not believe, and he will suffer much if he is not careful.'

'Then tell me, and I'll do what I can to help,' Jenny said determinedly.

'Peter Blaine is doing his best to harm Craig, in many ways. He told me bad things about you and Craig to make me jealous and angry, hoping that I would help him.'

'He told me you were living with Craig,' Jenny countered, and saw anger flare in the girl's dark eyes. 'But why is he trying to cause trouble for Craig?'

'He wants to take over Craig's business interests, especially the estate on Panaga, which Craig was prepared to sell until you came to the island. Now you are standing in a dead woman's shoes, and if you are not careful you'll end up the same way Ann Hannant did.'

Jenny shook her head. 'I find it hard to believe that Peter Blaine had anything to do with Ann Hannant's death,' she said. 'That was just talk!'

'Blaine had nothing to do with her death!' Aya said.

'Was the death accidental?'

'I cannot speak on the matter. I am here only to help you keep Craig out of trouble.' Aya's voice faltered, and she paused before continuing. 'I love Craig, and I've always hoped he could love me, but he never even looked at me. Now you've turned up and he's interested only in you!' She sighed heavily. 'I have finally accepted that he will never love me. But I have let Blaine think I still have hopes because he wants to use my jealousy for his own ends, and if I go along with him, I might be able to discover his plans, which I will tell you.'

'Does Craig know anything at all about this?'

'No. And it would not help if we told him.'

'All right,' Jenny nodded. 'Then we'll keep this to ourselves, but you must be very careful, Aya! Peter Blaine is a determined man. If he ever suspected that you were betraying him you would be in a lot of trouble.'

'I know how to handle Blaine.' Aya got to her feet. 'I'll call you when I have something to tell you. Good-bye.'

'Good-bye,' Jenny replied, and watched the girl hurry away before returning to the hospital and a hastily-eaten lunch.

The afternoon seemed to drag because of her impatience to see Craig, and although she was kept busy, Jenny had time to think about the situation. Worry clung to the darker recesses of her mind, and when it was time to go off duty she hurried out to the street and looked around for Craig, sighing heavily in relief when she found him waiting in his car.

'Hello,' he called, getting out of the car and coming to meet her. 'Hey, you must be growing accustomed to the routine because you don't look as tired as you did after your first day.'

'I'm all right now, thanks,' she responded. 'Have you had a good day?'

'Very good. I've finished checking the boat, and if you're not too tired I'd like to take a trip around the island to test the engine.'

'That sounds great.' Jenny nodded eagerly. 'I could do with some fresh air.'

He helped her into the car, and she tingled at the touch of his hand. She sat motionless beside him, thankful that nothing untoward had happened during the day. But when he drove out of town, Jenny frowned.

'Where's the boat?' she enquired.

'It's moored at my jetty in the cove. It's easier to work on there. I want the engine running right because when you do finish at the hospital I'm going to take you back to Panaga for an extended visit. You liked it there, and I think we should spend a couple of days away, where the hospital can't send for you if they decide they need you again. You did like Panaga, didn't you?'

'Very much.' She caught a glimpse of the bay as they reached the road that skirted it, and suddenly realised the wind was very strong, the sea much rougher than usual. 'Is there a storm brewing?' she demanded.

'The glass is down and there are reports of a storm tomorrow,' he said casually. 'You're not worried by choppy water, are you?'

'No.' She spoke bravely, keeping doubt out of her tone. 'But I can't help wondering what the passage through the reef will be like. It's fierce on the calmest day.'

'Strangely enough, it doesn't get much worse in a storm,' he replied. 'It's probably as rough as it can get. Are you through at the hospital yet?'

She shook her head. 'Another day, I think.'

Craig drove down into the cove and parked behind his big warehouse by the jetty. The wind thrust at Jenny as she alighted from the car, and her doubts increased as they walked to where the motor cruiser was bobbing and tugging at its mooring.

'You have to trust the engine to keep going when you negotiate the reef, don't you?' she asked, broaching the subject uppermost in her mind. 'What would happen if it stopped at a crucial moment?'

Craig laughed. 'The boat would smash itself to pieces on the reef, and no-one could expect to escape alive. It's that dangerous! But only if the boat is unreliable and you have a skipper less experienced than me.' He shook his head. 'Sorry! I'm joking again! It's a weakness of mine! There's nothing to worry about. I personally check over the engine every week, and so far I've had no trouble and never lost a passenger.'

Jenny suppressed a shiver of doubt as he helped her on to the shuddering deck of the motor cruiser, and he glanced at her taut expression and laughed as he put an arm around her shoulder.

'I was just kidding,' he said softly. 'These marine engines never fail. And if we had any trouble out there, I expect I could get us through without power, so don't worry about a thing.'

'All right,' she responded. 'I have every confidence in you.'

He started the engine and then stepped ashore to cast off. When he came back to the wheel, he edged the craft away from the jetty before steering it through ninety degrees and setting course for the distant reef. Jenny watched his every movement, enamoured by the sight of him. His face was rugged, bronzed in the evening sunlight, and his eyes were keen and bright. He looked at her suddenly, then pointed away to starboard, and she followed the direction of his pointing finger to see another motor cruiser heading in the same direction as themselves.

'That's Blaine's boat,' Craig said, 'and he means to beat us to the reef.'

'Can we beat him?' Jenny demanded.

Craig grinned. 'You don't think I'm going to let him show off in front of you, do you? Hold tight.'

He advanced the throttle and a powerful roar hammered Jenny's ear-drums. The craft leaped forward and sped towards the reef. Jenny clung desperately to a stanchion, her pulses racing with excitement. She looked at Blaine's boat, saw a large wake boiling up from its stern, and glanced at Craig.

'Can he beat us?' she demanded. 'He has a bigger boat.'

Craig glanced at the other craft, then looked ahead at the reef, his eyes narrowed in calculation. 'It'll be close,' he judged. 'But we won't give in without a fight.' He notched the throttle wider, and Jenny clung to her support with all the strength she could muster as the boat shuddered and crashed through the ever-growing waves.

The two boats drew closer together as their courses converged upon the one narrow channel through the reef, and Jenny laughed aloud through sheer excitement when she judged that Craig was having the best of the race. She could see three figures aboard Blaine's boat, and a tingle ran through her when she recognised Blaine's face as he turned to check their progress.

'We've got him,' Craig said exultantly. 'His boat may be bigger but his engine isn't more powerful and he hasn't got our speed. Now hang on. I want to hit top speed to draw ahead of him, but I must throttle down before we reach the passage or I won't have the necessary control to fight through.'

'Be careful, Craig!' Jenny warned. 'Don't do anything rash!'

'You don't think I'd risk your neck just to show Blaine a clean stern, do you?' he countered.

'I wouldn't put it past you!' she replied, and he chuckled.

She watched in rapt fascination as the boats drew even closer together, and Blaine's craft was half a length ahead. But Craig coaxed more speed from his engine and the boat seemed to bounce from one wave top to the next. They slowly drew level with the larger boat, and Jenny was breathless as she stared into Blaine's dark face across a dozen feet of rough water.

Craig started to pull ahead.

'You're beating him, Craig!' she yelled, her eyes wide with excitement.

'I told you we could!' He did not look at her now, his concentration fixed upon what he was doing.

The thunderous roar of the waves ahead battered Jenny's ears and seemed to fill the universe. She swayed and rolled to the motion of the boat, her hands fastened to the stanchion in a death-like grip. Laughter bubbled from her lips in sheer exhilaration. Blaine's boat was fast losing its station on their starboard side, and Craig was steering to the right, easing to a course that would take them safely through the gap in the reef. He throttled down suddenly and the boat faltered, seemed to stand still after their mad race to the reef. Blaine was well and truly beaten, already dropping back to second place, and Jenny was overjoyed when Craig turned and mockingly saluted the trailing boat.

Craig set a more leisurely pace and they had a wonderful time exploring some of the inlets that dotted the northern part of the coast. He showed her how to steer and control the boat, and Jenny had never been happier. She felt very close to Craig in those intimate moments, and sensed that he was falling in love with her, believing that his every action and glance pointed to the fact, and her own feelings blossomed wildly.

All too soon, they had to turn back, and it was almost dark when they ran the gauntlet of the reef on the inward trip. They found the calm water in the bay without incident and made for the shore. When she stepped on to the shadowed jetty, Jenny was sorry that the evening had ended.

'Well!' Craig declared as they walked to his car. 'Wasn't that an ideal way to spend an evening? I'll bet you forgot all about the hospital while we were afloat.'

'I certainly did!' she agreed. 'I've never known such excitement. And wasn't it good to push Peter Blaine into second place?'

'I thoroughly enjoyed it,' Craig admitted. 'But tell me, how do you feel about your new way of life? Are you glad you came to Taminga?'

'I wish I could have made the decision years ago,' she responded, and a sad note touched her voice as she added, 'Everything would have been so good.'

He slid an arm around her, drawing her close in the velvet darkness, and she became breathless with anticipation, instinctively turning her face up to him.

His features were a blur in the shadows as he stood powerful and tall before her, with stars twinkling in the sky at his back. Then he bent his head and his mouth found her lips, their contact filling her with passion. The night was silent and still, and she could smell the sea as the breeze blew inland, while the sound of the breakers out across the darkened bay was so natural in the background, that she hardly noticed it.

'You must be very tired,' he said when he released her. 'I should have realised. You've been hard at work all day and should have rested this evening.'

'Don't you believe it!' she countered. 'I wouldn't have missed this evening for anything!'

8

When Jenny awoke the next morning, it was to see the palm trees shaking vigorously under a gale-force wind, and her heart faltered when she looked toward the reef and saw gigantic waves battering it. It was a fearsome scene, the sea aroused to awesome power, and she could imagine what the gap through the reef would be like at this moment.

When she went into the kitchen Debbie was there, and Tim was on the point of leaving. He looked intently at her, saw her happiness, and went off with a smile. Jenny sat down, breathing deeply as she took stock of the situation.

'I heard you come in last night,' Debbie said. 'You were quite late!'

'I got off duty about seven, and Craig took me out in his boat. That was why I was late in.'

'Great! I was thinking you were being overworked at the hospital! Did you have a nice time?'

'Wonderful! It was such a relief to get some fresh air!'

'Haven't they finished with you yet at the hospital?'

'This might be the last day. I hope so, anyway. I need the rest of my holiday.' Jenny sighed. 'I hope you don't mind the way Craig is monopolising my free time, Debbie. We had planned to do so much together, hadn't we? And there's poor Selina! I've hardly seen her since the day I arrived! And she was so looking forward to being with me. We haven't even been swimming yet!'

'Don't worry about that!' Debbie smiled. 'If you're happy, then that's all that matters. In fact, I'd rather you saw Craig than me!' She paused. 'I don't mean that exactly how it sounded. What I mean is, you're the best thing that could have happened to Craig, and I'm sure he's right for you.'

164

Jenny nodded, and she was thoughtful until Craig arrived. He came striding into the kitchen, filling the doorway when he paused, and seeing him in sober daylight gave her the chance to study him critically. It was obvious he was a changed man. He laughed easily, his face was less strained, and his eyes were bright and filled with awareness. She recalled the first time they met, and hardly recognised him as being the same man. He had quite evidently found a new purpose in life.

Craig drove her to the hospital, and when he drew up at the gate she was reluctant to leave him, and it showed. His eyes were gleaming when he looked across at her.

'What's on your agenda today?' she enquired.

'Some work to do on the boat. I want to get it done in case this is your last day on duty. If it is then I'd like to push off for Panaga tomorrow. Would that be all right with you?'

'Certainly!' Her pulses quickened. 'But how long will this storm last? You won't try to get to Panaga by sea while it's so rough, will you?'

'The short answer is no!' He smiled. 'I wouldn't risk it with you aboard, although you proved last evening that you're as reckless as me.'

She laughed at the recollection of the previous evening, but wanted more information on his plans, and added:

'You said something yesterday about staying on Panaga for a few days.'

'Yes, there's a lot you didn't see on your first visit, and I'm keen to be your personal guide.'

She smiled. 'I was thrilled that first time, so I can hardly wait for the second trip out.'

'Well, just make sure you get finished here today.' He glanced at the hospital. 'I've missed your company a great deal during the last few days, although I've managed to get through a mountain of work. Are the nurses all getting over their sickness?'

'Yes. Sister Mayhew should be back today, and if no-one else goes sick then I can resume my holiday tomorrow. It hasn't been too bad, has it? At least the ice has been broken as far as work is concerned, and I shan't feel such a stranger when I come back after my holiday.' She smiled. 'I must go. I'll see you at the usual time this evening.'

'Let me know if anything changes,' he said, leaning sideways and kissing her cheek. 'You might be able to get away early! I'll be on the boat most of the day and you can reach me by telephone.'

Jenny watched him drive away, her heart going with him. Then she turned and entered the hospital, carrying in her mind a picture of his face . . .

Sister Mayhew was back on duty, Jenny discovered. Her superior was tall and slender, a blonde of about thirty-five who was strikingly attractive. Jenny recalled that Debbie had said the sister was in love with Frank Carter! Barbara Mayhew greeted Jenny cheerfully, although she was still feeling the effects of her illness.

'I've heard a great deal about you, Nurse,' she said, 'all of it good. It was fortunate you were able to come in as you did, but we're getting back to normal now and you should be able to resume your holiday tomorrow, if you wish.'

'Thank you, Sister. That will be fine,' Jenny replied in a matter-of-fact tone, although she was greatly relieved by the news.

'You won't be worked so hard today,' the sister continued. 'And it's a pity you didn't get a more pleasant introduction to life on the island.'

'It was an emergency, and that's the way a crisis develops.' Jenny could now feel fatalistic about it. 'I'm relieved your staff are much better.'

Sister Mayhew nodded, and gave Jenny instructions for the morning routine. Jenny thought of Craig, of how pleased he would be to learn that she would be off duty again, and she threw herself into her work in happy abandon.

The worries of the past few days had miraculously faded, and her hopes knew no bounds, until she went to the canteen for coffee and saw Peter Blaine in the corridor, apparently waiting to see her.

'I trust you had a pleasant evening yesterday,' he said crisply.

'I did, as a matter of fact.' She smiled at her recollection of the race for the gap in the reef, and could tell by his expression that he was still smarting about the way he had been beaten. She wished she could think of something apt to say.

'You were very lucky to survive that idiotic race!' he said harshly. 'I wouldn't have trusted myself to Hannant's navigation.'

'Craig is a marvellous seaman! He didn't do a thing wrong, and he can certainly handle a boat.'

'I could have beaten him to the gap but I didn't want to risk harming you! If anyone went overboard they couldn't last two minutes in that rough water. I

169

think Hannant is a reckless, overgrown schoolboy who shouldn't be allowed to sail a boat or drive a car.'

Jenny looked into his dark gaze and controlled her thoughts, not wishing to put her opinion of him into words or inflame him with a retort.

'I suppose it's useless asking you to see me again,' he said.

'That's right!' She nodded emphatically.

'He's put a spell on you!' Blaine nodded slowly. 'But it won't last. You'll see him for what he is before very long.'

'There must be something basically wrong with me, because I like him a lot, despite what you say about him,' she said quietly. 'Now if you'll excuse me! I am very busy!' She walked around him and continued, and when she had put some distance between them she glanced over her shoulder to see that he was motionless, watching her intently. She suppressed a shiver. There had been an intangible expression in Blaine's eyes that could easily have given her nightmares, she thought.

Later, she was called to the office for a telephone call, and her pulses raced as she imagined that it would be Craig. However, it was Aya who spoke in her ear, and Jenny tensed, anticipating trouble.

'Can I talk to you now, over the telephone?' the girl asked.

'Not really.' Jenny frowned, for Sister Mayhew was seated only feet away.

'Then I must see you during your break.' Aya laughed, an unmusical sound that scraped on Jenny's nerves. 'I'm afraid I said something to Peter Blaine that must have upset him.'

'Oh, dear!' Jenny compressed her lips. 'I can see you at about half past twelve. Would that be convenient?'

'I'll be there,' Aya said, and rang off.

Jenny went back to work, worried by the telephone call. What had Aya said to Blaine? Why had she antagonised him? She fought her impatience until she eventually took her break and hurried out ot the hospital gate.

Aya was already waiting, impatiently pacing the pavement, and Jenny drew a deep breath as the girl looked up, saw her, and came hurrying forward.

'What's wrong, Aya?' she demanded.

'I had to telephone Blaine this morning,' the girl replied. 'He wanted a report on my progress in driving a wedge between you and Craig. He was in a very bad mood. He'd seen you here and you made him angry.'

'And what did you tell him?'

'The truth! I thought it would be better to let him know that he had no chance to get you away from Craig. I told him you and Craig are in love and would probably marry. Afterwards, I was sorry I said it, because he was so angry and said he would have to use other measures to part you. I asked him what I could do to help because I need to find out what he plans.'

'Are you sure he trusts you?'

'He does. He told me to fix Craig's boat so it breaks down the next time it goes through the reef!'

Jenny froze in horror. 'You're joking!' she gasped.

Aya regarded her with unblinking eyes and Jenny suppressed a shudder.

'You wouldn't do that, would you?' she asked fearfully.

Aya laughed bitterly. 'I would rather kill myself than harm one hair of Craig's head,' she said sharply. 'I'd do anything to save him from trouble, and Blaine doesn't realise that!'

Jenny shook her head. 'This is so shocking! What can we do? Wouldn't it be better to report it to the police?'

'It would be my word against Blaine's!' Aya shrugged fatalistically. 'You know who they would believe! Blaine is an influential man on the island.'

'But how do you know Blaine won't do something you can't know about?' Jenny asked fearfully.

'Because I have agreed to do his dirty work for him.' Aya smiled. 'I know about your trip to Panaga. You're probably going tomorrow. I told Blaine to gain his confidence, and now I have to fix the boat so an accident occurs when it is passing through the rough water of the reef.'

'But I'll be aboard!' Jenny suppressed a shudder. 'Does Blaine want me dead as well?' she demanded.

'He means to be out there in his boat to pick you up! That would make him seem like a hero in your eyes. And he would leave Craig in the water to drown.'

'But this is dreadful!' Jenny stared at the girl, shock blurring her eyes. 'What can we do, Aya? Surely Craig will have to be told now!'

'No!' The girl shook her head emphatically. 'That would not help at all. There would be no proof, and if we stop Blaine carrying out his plan this time he will do something in the future without letting me know. But I have a way of stopping Mr Blaine so just leave it to me. Don't worry about it.'

'I can't help worrying!' Jenny's brow

was furrowed as she thought over what had been said, and in the back of her mind she could only wonder if Aya was to be trusted. But she had no option but to go along with the girl, she realised. There was nothing she could do alone. 'What can be done to stop Blaine?' she asked.

'He will be stopped,' Aya nodded grimly. 'But don't ask me how. You don't think I would let anything happen to Craig, do you?' She smiled, her dark eyes filled with an unholy light. 'When you go to Panaga there will be nothing wrong with Craig's boat. And Blaine thinks I will not disobey his orders. And he is right. I will fix a boat! But if it is not Craig's, then whose will it be?' She laughed in a low, grating tone, and Jenny shivered.

'Aya, you don't mean you'll do something to Blaine's boat!' she gasped.

'I don't mean anything! Just don't worry about it. This is not England, remember, and sometimes one has to give the law a push.'

'I can't accept that!' Jenny shook her head emphatically. 'We'll have to tell Craig about this and leave him to deal with it. He has a right to know because it's his life that's being threatened.'

'If you say anything to Craig then he will do the wrong thing! Please do as I say. I have told you this to put you on your guard, but that is as far as it goes. Blaine is setting this trap, and it's only right that he should be the one to suffer. He won't drown, if that's what is worrying you! He is too good a swimmer to die like that. But Craig will be saved, and the lesson might force Blaine to forget his evil plot.'

Jenny glanced at her watch, her mind burdened with worry. Aya smiled briefly and turned away.

'I must go,' she said. 'I have to watch Craig now, just in case. It would be a mistake to trust Blaine an inch.'

Jenny stared after the-girl, filled with a seriousness that frightened her. Peter Blaine was actually plotting to kill Craig! She sighed. What could be done about that? She just could not leave it all to Aya, and common sense suggested that she warn Craig of the danger!

She returned to the hospital, staggering as the wind caught her unawares and almost knocked her over. She glanced around, and was surprised by the intensity of the gathering storm. Looking up at the sky, she saw huge, black clouds scudding before the wind, and a shiver of apprehension went through her.

When she went back on duty, nurses were closing the windows, and the heavy panes were rattling furiously in protest at the invisible onslaughts of the wind. There was a stifling atmosphere which seemed to constrict the throat, and Jenny's worries increased. There was a nervousness inside her which had never been apparent before, and she could not shrug it off. Twice she decided to call Craig and explain what was going on, but each time she reached the phone she had second thoughts, deciding it would be better to rely on Aya. The girl obviously had Craig's best interests at heart and would surely not let anything untoward happen to him.

The afternoon seemed never-ending, and Jenny was practically at her wit's end when Frank Carter suddenly appeared on the ward. He came to her, smiling.

'Jenny, you can resume your holiday tomorrow,' he said, 'and I want to thank you for helping us out this week. I don't know how we would have managed if you hadn't been around. We're very much in your debt, and if there's any way I can ever repay you then just mention it.'

'Thank you, Doctor, but that's all right,' she replied, wishing she could ask for help with Craig. 'I'm glad I was available.'

'We haven't enough nurses of your calibre here, more's the pity,' he continued. 'Thanks again. And enjoy what's left of your holiday. We'll see you again when you come back.'

'Thank you.' Jenny went on with her work. This part of her life was settling down fine, but her nerves were protesting at the strain of wondering what to do about Blaine. The whole thing seemed so unreal, but when she pictured Blaine's face and recalled the hard gleam she had seen in his eyes earlier she knew the plot was not so fantastic . . .

When it was finally time to go off duty she could not leave the wards and change out of uniform quickly enough. Hurrying out of the hospital, she halted in shock, for rain was falling in torrents and the wind had strengthened even more. She stood sheltering in the hospital doorway, peering for Craig's car. But it was not in the usual place and she stared at the spot, her fears activated.

Glancing at her watch, she realised that she was several minutes earlier than usual, and drew a deep breath to steady herself. She wanted to avoid

179

looking perturbed when Craig arrived because he was so observant. She took a fresh grip on her nerves and forced herself to calm down.

'Jenny!' a voice called at her back, and she turned to see Frank Carter peering out through the half opened doorway. 'There's a telephone call for you. You can take it in my office.'

'Thank you!' She caught her breath nervously as she hurried behind him back into the hospital, and her heart thudded as she wondered if something else had gone wrong.

'Help yourself.' Doctor Carter paused at the open door of his office. 'I've got rounds to make. Just close the door when you leave.'

Jenny nodded, almost overcome with fear as she sat down at the desk and picked up the telephone receiver.

'Hello,' she said huskily, her pulses racing. Her throat was dry and constricted, and she wondered just how much more tension she could take.

'This is Aya! I'm at the boathouse in

the cove. You must come quickly, Jenny. Craig is about to put to sea in this storm and I can't talk him out of it.'

'What?' Jenny was devastated. 'Why does he want to go out now?'

'Blaine was just here and he and Craig had an argument about who was the better seaman. They had some kind of a race last evening, didn't they? Well, Craig is going out in the storm to prove he can get through the reef in bad weather. Blaine said it's impossible but Craig just laughed at him.'

'But Craig isn't a fool!' Jenny gasped. 'He must know if he can make it or not. He said the gap through the reef doesn't get much worse in a storm. It's normally as bad as it can get.'

'I've been trying to talk Craig out of it but he won't listen. He's been drinking, and I don't think he's fit to handle the boat in good weather, let alone the storm. You've got to do something, Jenny.'

'Can you delay him until I get there?' Jenny asked. 'I'm leaving the hospital now. I'll get a taxi to the jetty.'

'I'll do what I can, but you must hurry!' Aya said. 'Craig has already pushed me out of his office. He will soon be ready to go, and I know he'll never survive the weather coming into the bay.'

'I'm on my way,' Jenny said sharply, her thoughts already leaping ahead of the situation. 'Do whatever you can to delay him, Aya.'

9

The taxi left town and followed the coast road north before descending a steep incline into the cove, and to Jenny the trip seemed interminable as she peered through the streaming windscreen at the road ahead, her mind frozen as she thought of Craig. And she prayed she would be in time to stop him taking his life into his hands.

They finally reached the Hannant warehouse beside the long, wooden pier that jutted out like a black finger into the bay. Rain was pouring down, making visibility difficult, and Jenny hurriedly paid the driver and stepped out into the rain. She drew a deep breath as she looked around to get her bearings, and the first thing she saw was Craig's motor cruiser lying moored to the jetty some fifty yards away. A sigh gusted from her and she was overcome with relief.

The sky was heavy with dark clouds, and the blasting wind tugged and pulled at her, almost knocking her off balance with its blustery strength. Her feet slipped on the treacherously wet boards of the jetty, and she narrowed her eyes in the deceptive half-light when she fancied she saw a dark figure moving about on the deck of the boat.

At least she was not too late! Now she could warn Craig of the danger. As she reached the boat she stumbled over a mooring line and nearly plunged into the bay, catching her left knee on the rail of the boat as she lurched sideways. Her clutching fingers caught hold of the rail and she managed to haul herself into the stern cockpit. Breathless and shaking, she looked around for Craig, but the craft now seemed deserted.

Thrusting open the door that led below, she called out urgently, 'Craig, are you aboard?'

Her voice echoed mockingly in the silence, and she stepped through the doorway into the companionway, staggering when the boat rolled under the thrust of a wave. She blundered forward, hands outstretched to save herself from falling. The door slammed at her back, and she gasped for breath as she leaned against the bulkhead.

It was quite dark inside the boat, and she narrowed her eyes, looking into the deserted galley on the left before turning to the doorway of the cabin. A frown touched her face when she found it empty, for she had seen a figure on the deck as she approached. She swung round to return to the stern cockpit, but as she seized hold of the door handle she heard a metallic, scraping sound, and froze, startled until she recognised it as a bolt sliding home on the outside of the door.

She grasped the handle and turned it, throwing her weight against the door. But it was immovable, and she leaned against it, pounding with her fist.

'Craig, are you out there?' she called, fighting a strand of fear which suddenly

185

unwound in the back of her mind. She listened intently, hearing nothing but the moaning of the wind and the lapping of waves against the hull. 'Craig, if it is you, then open the door. This is going beyond a joke.'

Again, silence followed the echoes of her voice, and she rattled the handle angrily, her patience fleeing. Her nerves were at breaking point and she had no reserves to call upon. Then she realised that it might not be Craig out there, and real fear began to flourish in her mind.

'Who's out there?' she demanded. 'Answer me.'

'Who do you think it is?' Aya's tone was triumphant, and when she laughed there was a trace of hysteria in her voice. 'I've got you trapped now, and I want you to know about it before you die.'

'Aya!' Jenny gasped in shock. 'What are you doing?'

'You need to ask?' The native girl laughed mockingly. 'Did you think I could stand by and watch Craig make a fool of himself over you after he did the same thing with his wife? And who do you think killed her? I did it! She was spoiling Craig's life, so I fixed her car and it went over the cliff. And I'll put you out of the way to stop Craig making the same mistake. You're not good for him.'

'Are you crazy?' Jenny pressed against the door. 'Where is Craig? I thought you said he was going to put to sea!'

'He's not that stupid! I made that up to get you down here. It's what Blaine planned, but he expects Craig to be with you, so he'll be surprised when he finds you alone. He's out there now, this side of the reef, waiting to pick you up and watch Craig drown. But it's his turn to die. He wanted me to fix this boat so it will break down, but I've fixed his so the engine will stop. Then he'll drift on to the reef, and you'll be with him.'

'Aya! You must listen to me!' Jenny said desperately. 'You're not helping Craig at all by doing this.'

'But I am! Blaine will be dead, and he's Craig's enemy. Now I'm casting you adrift, and if Blaine doesn't get to you, you'll die on the reef anyway!'

'Where is Craig?' Jenny called desperately.

'In the boathouse. I drugged him to keep him out of the way. Goodbye, English girl!'

'Please wait!' Jenny's heart was pounding. She listened intently but heard only the moaning of the wind. Her mind was reeling in shock. Aya had killed Craig's wife! And Blaine was out in the bay, waiting to pick her up, expecting Craig to be on the boat and determined to leave him to drown. She shook her head in disbelief, fighting down the fear that threatened to overcome her.

She slithered sideways as the boat lurched sickeningly, and the knowledge that Aya was casting her adrift shocked her into action. She looked around wildly. There had to be something she could do!

Recalling the evening when Craig

had taken her sailing, she remembered some of the things he had told her about the boat. She looked down, saw a small hatch in the floor, and reached for the metal ring let into it, pulling hard. The hatch came upwards, hinged on the left, and she peered down into the engine room. Breathing deeply, she dropped through the hatch into semi-darkness, and staggered violently as the craft began to pitch and roll. She was adrift! Aya had carried out her threat! She clenched her hands, fear filling her with desperation.

Going forward, she felt above her head for a hatch which gave access to the small foredeck, and her fingers encountered a bolt, which she withdrew with difficulty. But the hatch would not budge, and she felt around and discovered a second bolt. She had difficulty jerking it free, but it finally gave and she thrust against the hatch, which opened upwards and slammed back on the deck. Rain pelted in through the aperture, and Jenny uttered a silent prayer of relief as she grabbed the sides of the hatch and pulled herself upwards and out into the storm.

Sitting on the foredeck, she looked around quickly, and saw with stabbing fear that the boat had been cast adrift and was moving quite rapidly away from the shore. There was an indistinct figure standing on the jetty, and for a heart-stopping moment she thought it was Craig. But it was Aya, and, even as she recognised the girl, Aya turned away and ran to the boathouse in the background.

Jenny looked seaward, and was horrified by the sight that awaited her gaze. The reef was smothered with white water, and the never-ending roar of the crashing waves stunned her. Real darkness was beginning to creep into the evening, and the sky was burdened with ominous black clouds which hurled a ceaseless torrent of rain earthwards.

She got to her feet, and almost slipped over the side of the boat as it rolled. She grasped a rail and clung on desperately, feet hanging overboard, her entire weight suspended on her slender arms. For interminable moments she feared she would lose her hold and be swept away, but the boat suddenly pitched in the opposite direction and she managed to drag herself back to safety. Clinging to the rail, she worked her way over the roof of the cabin and slithered down into the comparative safety of the stern cockpit.

Her mind began working normally again, although she was deathly afraid. She looked towards the jetty to see it vanishing into the background as the tide carried the boat farther out into the bay. There was already a stretch of fifty yards of open water between the craft and the jetty, and it was widening with each passing second.

She turned to the controls and pressed the starter button as she had seen Craig do. But nothing happened! Gritting her teeth, she pressed the button again, her mind refusing to believe that the engine would not start.

But there was only a whirring sound and the engine did not fire. She flipped switches and desperately turned knobs on the control panel before pressing the button yet again. Still nothing happened, and a pang of despair stirred in her breast as she tried again and again without success.

The motion of the boat was becoming more violent, and she clung to a stanchion and paused to take stock. What else could she do? Could she swim back to the jetty? She looked at the ever-widening gap and shook her head. The water was too rough for her! She knew her limitations. She had to stick with the boat. She looked around despairingly and her desperate gaze alighted on a small locker. Jerking open the door, a gasp of relief escaped her when she saw signal flares, and was thankful that Craig had explained to her how they should be used. She ignited one, her heart pounding with trepidation, and peered upwards anxiously until a bright red flare burst high in the murk above the boat.

The wind howled around her, tugging at her wet clothes. She was unable to stand unaided, and clung to the stanchion to keep her balance while fear and despair vied for supremacy in her overburdened mind. The sound of the waves crashing on the reef seemed to have grown louder, and the beginnings of terror stabbed through her when she looked around and saw the boat was moving faster out into the bay, being inexorably drawn towards the tumult of the reef. The narrow gap in the reef that had frightened her when she passed through it with Craig was now almost non-existent, filled with flying spray and crashing water.

She looked shorewards, hardly able to see the jetty now. Everywhere was gloomy and there were no signs of life. She returned to the control panel and again tried to start the engine. If she could get some power she could save herself! The knowledge spurred her on, but there was not even a spark of life in the controls, and she did not know enough about the boat to find out what she was doing wrong.

She lifted her head suddenly, fancying that she had heard a shout cutting through the dull bluster of the storm. For a moment hope filled her. Had Craig become aware of her predicament and was on his way to save her? She looked around, and was startled to see a large boat coming towards her. Help was at hand! Her fear subsided and she gazed at the nearing boat, wide-eyed in relief. Then she realised it was Peter Blaine's vessel and disappointment filled her. But at least Blaine would be denied the fruition of his merciless plot.

Craig had managed to escape his clutches!

Blaine's figure became apparent at the helm in the stern cockpit, and a few moments later his boat slammed against the tossing derelict, the impact throwing Jenny to her knees. She clung to a rail, her hands fixed in a death-like grip, and stared at Blaine as he fastened his wheel with a short piece of rope and lunged across his stern to grasp the rail of Craig's boat, holding the two boats together, his head only feet away from Jenny.

'Quickly!' he yelled, his voice sounding puny, buffeted by the storm. 'Be quick and come aboard.'

Jenny listened to the insistent note of Blaine's engine, and, remembering Aya's words, shook her head. She had to gulp before she could speak, and then cried out in a shrill tone.

'Your boat isn't safe!' Her voice held a trace of terror. 'Come aboard and try to start this engine.'

'There's nothing wrong with my boat!' came the quick reply. 'Yours is in distress, and you'll be on the reef in a few minutes.'

'You're a fool!' Jenny shouted. 'You trusted Aya to do your dirty work but she loves Craig, and she's fixed your boat to break down.'

Blaine's change of expression would have been comical in any other situation as Jenny's words sank into his consciousness. For a moment he gazed at her, the two boats rocking in unison. Then he half-turned and looked at his own vessel, cocking his head to listen to the note of the engine. He looked at Jenny again, shaking his head in disbelief, and at that moment his engine spluttered and fell silent.

'I told you so!' Jenny shouted. 'For heaven's sake come aboard while there's still time!'

Blaine stared at her for what seemed endless moments, while the two boats plunged and rolled in the rough sea. He was still shaking his head, Jenny noticed, and then he released his hold upon the rail of Craig's boat and slithered back into his own cockpit. A gap quickly opened up between the two boats, and Jenny watched in frozen horror as they parted. He was leaving her! The knowledge evoked a cry of terror from her.

She saw Blaine making frantic efforts to restart his engine, but nothing happened and the boats continued to drift apart. Then Blaine straightened and looked around. Jenny watched him dully. He glanced towards the reef, turned his head to survey the distant shore, and the next instant was galvanised into action. He shrugged out of his jacket, and she watched in amazement as he pulled off his shirt and then removed his shoes. He looked at her across the widening gap between the two boats, his face set in harsh lines, his mouth agape. Then he drew a deep breath and jumped upon the stern of his boat, where he paused for a split second before diving into the surging sea.

Jenny gulped, not daring to believe her worst thoughts. Surely he was trying to swim towards her! He must know the only chance was to get Craig's boat started! She saw his head bobbing on the waves, and was sickened by fear when she realised he had turned his back on her. He was intent upon swimming ashore, concerned only with his own life! He had callously abandoned her to the mercy of the waves!

Jenny sank down on the floor of the cockpit, despair robbing her of determination. This was hopeless. She was going to die in this terrifying storm because the only man who could save her was lying drugged and helpless ashore. Moments passed and the boat pitched and tossed alarmingly as the waves grew bigger the nearer they drifted towards the reef. She realised there was nothing more to be done.

The faint sound of a powerful engine suddenly impressed itself upon her ears and she stiffened, thinking she was imagining the sound. She got to her knees and peered around while the sound grew louder. Standing up, she was filled with renewed hope, and suddenly there was movement out there in the murk. A squat, black shape dashed into view and came speeding towards her, its small bow wave crinkling whitely and a high wake boiling and threshing at its stern.

An inshore rescue boat! Jenny stared as if it had come from another planet.

She had forgotten about the flare she sent up! Someone must have seen and reported it! She could see two dark figures in the craft, and watched mesmerised as it sped around the stricken cruiser and then came darting in beside it. One of the men arose and hurled himself upwards, strong hands grasping the rail, and Jenny watched as he swung himself aboard and dropped in a heap beside her. His pale face turned towards her, and she was amazed when she suddenly recognised Craig.

He pushed himself upright and grasped her, lifting and carrying her towards the cabin. He put her hands around a rail and she gripped instinctively. For a moment he peered into her face, then bent and kissed her cheek. She watched him as he turned to the controls, shaking her head in despair because, although he had come to save her, he had merely placed himself firmly into the trap that had been set for him . . .

The engine fired and roared powerfully, and Jenny gasped in shock. What had he done? How had he managed it? She shook herself from her fear and reeled towards him. He was concentrating on their position, spinning the wheel to bring the bows of the craft around. The awful pitching and rolling lessened immediately, and as Craig opened the throttle the boat countered the pull of the currents and began to move back towards the jetty.

Jenny fell against Craig and he put a protective arm around her. She looked up at him, saw his grim face and set jaw, and her fear evaporated.

'What did you do to the engine?' she demanded, her voice sounding puny against the storm. 'I tried everything to get it to start but nothing happened!'

He smiled despite the gravity of the situation, and looked down into her upturned face. His arm was like a steel band about her, and Jenny threw her arms around him, assailed by nervous reaction. He kissed her again, and she choked on the rush of emotion that constricted her throat. She felt safe in his embrace and clung to him as if she would never let go.

'You didn't turn on the fuel,' he said. 'Look!' he moved slightly and pointed to a metal pipe fixed to the side of the boat. 'See this lever? It was pointing up at a right angle to the pipe, which is the 'off' position. It has to be put parallel to the pipe to enable the fuel to reach the engine.'

'I would have been killed if you hadn't arrived!' Jenny gasped. 'Why didn't I get it right?'

'Never mind!' He held her tightly. 'I'm here now and the danger is past. I told you I'm a good sailor, and I've been out in worse weather than this.'

'You said you're the best!' she contradicted. 'And now I believe you! But how have you managed to get here? Aya said she drugged you.' Jenny clung to him as if she feared he might suddenly vanish.

He nodded grimly. 'She attempted it, and if Blaine hadn't tried it when he did, I wouldn't have recognised the taste and stopped drinking before it could really knock me out. As it was, I was hardly aware of what I was doing for some time, and it wasn't until Aya came into the boathouse after setting you adrift that I could begin to put two and two together. When I questioned her, she told me the whole story about Blaine and his plot. I locked her in the boathouse, and as I came out to the jetty to look for you, I saw your flare going up. I called the Inshore Rescue and asked Tom Whittaker to come and collect me, and here we are.'

He needed only half his attention on the boat now, and Jenny looked up into his face. He smiled, his eyes gleaming. She watched him intently, her sense of relief almost too keen to bear as fear and tension dropped away from her. Then she remembered Peter Blaine, and dropped her head against his chest as she explained what had happened.

Craig uttered an imprecation and reached out for his radio telephone. He called up Tom Whittaker in the inshore rescue craft, giving instructions, and Jenny narrowed her eyes as she tried to watch the progress of the little craft when it darted off to make a search.

'There's a small searchlight on the bow,' Craig said. 'I can operate it from here, but you'll have to help me look for Blaine. We'll make a sweep across the bay, but I fear he won't make it, strong swimmer that he is, because there's so much spray it would asphyxiate a swimmer.'

Craig switched on the searchlight and Jenny stared intently at the angry waves while they moved back and forth, creeping ever nearer to the shore as they searched the area Blaine would have covered. The inshore rescue boat zipped by them a couple of times, covering an overlapping area, the radio telephone crackling with Whittaker's voice, until a sudden exclamation sounded. Then Whittaker reported seeing a body floating face down in the water and they waited anxiously for what seemed like an age until the voice sounded again.

'I've got him aboard, Craig. It's Peter Blaine all right, and he's dead. I'm going in now. See you when you get back to shore.'

'Thank you, Tom,' Craig replied. 'We're all right now!'

Jenny suppressed a sigh as she watched the little rescue boat dart away and become lost to sight. Peter Blaine was dead, she thought dully, but if he had succeeded in his terrible plot, it would have been Craig lying dead in that little boat. She shuddered, and Craig switched off the searchlight and put a comforting arm around her slender shoulders.

'Jenny, for some minutes back there I was afraid I'd lost you,' he said softly, his lips close to her ear, 'and it made me realise that I love you. I fell in love with you that first moment we met, although I admit that at first I tried to fight against my feelings because of my past experiences, but when it came down to life and death, everything became crystal clear. I love you, Jenny, and I hope my suspicions about you are correct.'

'Your suspicions?' she queried.

'That you're in love with me!' He paused and watched her face.

She nodded joyously. 'You're a very perceptive man, among other things,' she replied. 'I do love you, Craig. And I've known it for some time. What happened today merely proved it.'

Craig kissed her, cutting off her words, and she relaxed in his embrace. The boat broached a little, and Craig pulled away for a moment, looking around quickly and spinning the wheel to correct their course.

'Poor girl!' Craig commented. 'You're soaking wet and shivering! You've been put in fear of your life, Jenny, yet you can stand here calm and collected and make a firm decision about your future life.'

'My future?' she repeated.

'You said you love me, and you know my feelings. You can put two and two together quite skilfully, so how do you sum up this situation?'

She looked into his eyes and a sigh of relief escaped her. Craig was smiling gently, completely at home in this terrible environment. But she no longer felt even a tremor of fear, and knew it was because she was with him. She nodded, aware that he did not need an answer to his question, for he drew her even closer into his arms and kissed her tenderly while she responded eagerly, her cares and doubts falling away like a discarded cloak. The storm would abate eventually, she told herself. Sunlight would return to the island, and when it came, the sinister shadows that had lain in the background, would no longer exist.

She nodded happily, aware that the future would be fine in many ways . . .

THE END

TRUST IN ME

Rena George

When Kerra Morrison is named main beneficiary in her uncle's will, her cousins Sarah and David are furious their father favoured her over them. So when someone attempts to sabotage Kerra's new tearoom, her cousins seem to be the obvious culprits. But are there darker forces at work? The town's GP, Dr Duncan Crombie, comes to her aid. It would be easy to fall for such a man — if he didn't keep throwing up barriers every time they seem to be getting close . . .

DANGEROUS AFFAIR

Irena Nieslony

Feisty Eve Masters has had enough of the rat race. A successful career in London has allowed her to retire at forty-three and move to Crete. There, she falls for the handsome, but quiet, David Baker — but despite the mutual attraction, theirs is a volatile relationship. However, this is not the only thing to keep Eve occupied. The day she arrives, an English ex-pat estate agent is found murdered. Eve is intent on solving the crime — putting her own life in danger . . .